# Junebug and the Body

### By Robert D. Bennett

Publisher
Rebellion Books
www.RebellionBooks.com

## ACKNOWLEDGEMENTS

For Robert, who used to carry junebugs in his mouth so they could tickle his tongue. He was the inspiration for the name. Also, to my Uncle Bobby who I always picture when I think of Uncle Jasper and to his wife Aunt Sarah.

And, as always, for the others in my family who have and do encourage me in every way.

# CHAPTER 1

I can honestly say the summer of 1974 was the most exciting one in my life.

It all started when we found the body.

\*\*\*\*\*\*\*\*\*\*\*\*\*\*\*\*\*\*\*\*\*\*\*\*\*\*

I'd come to live with Uncle Jasper and Aunt Sarah when I was five years old, not long after my daddy died in Vietnam and my momma got killed in a car wreck.

The little town of St. John was a lot different than Houston, where I'd been living, but it was where my daddy had grown up and I got used to the pine covered hills of East Texas pretty quick.

Uncle Jasper and Aunt Sarah were always nice to me, but at first you could tell they weren't used to kids. Sometimes, after I'd done something that she got particularly excited about, Aunt Sarah would get this expression on her face like she thought I was two sandwiches short of having a full picnic. A good example of this was the time I caught the garter snake and put it in the pocket of my pants, promptly forgetting about it. The real problem was caused by Aunt Sarah's habit of going through the pockets of my clothes before she put them in the washing machine, a practice developed after six or eight of my crayons had gotten washed along with a load of her dresses. Anyway, me and Uncle Jasper were in the back yard digging worms for a fishing trip when we heard Aunt Sarah scream. We tore into the house and saw her in the utility room holding a broom and jumping back and forth like she was afraid to stand in one place too long. I guessed what had happened and asked Uncle Jasper in a whisper if I should tell her it was just a garter snake, but he just put his hand on my shoulder and shook his head. We both backed out of the kitchen and finished our worm gathering.

I never did see that snake again.

Uncle Jasper is a long, lanky man, prone to wearing his hair slicked back with Vitalis and usually seen in short sleeved coveralls with his sheriff's badge pinned to the front. He fought in World War II but doesn't talk about it much. On Memorial and Veterans Day he can usually be counted on to take his old uniform out of the closet and wear it in the parade with the other members of the V.F.W.

When I was younger I didn't care much for Uncle Jasper, mainly because he seemed to delight in tormenting me about the size of my feet. I knew good and well they weren't long enough to snow ski on, even though I don't remember ever actually seeing a snow ski.

After I got a little older the kidding quit bothering me, and now I kind of worry when he doesn't do it because that means he's got something on his mind. Unfortunately, it's almost always some new job for me to do. If there is one thing I hate it's work that "builds character". To hear him tell it when he was a kid the only time they weren't working was when they were walking to school through the snow. One of these days I've got to make it a point to ask Miss Bunion, my teacher, what happened to make it so much warmer now than when Uncle Jasper was a kid.

If I were to look in a crowd of women and try to figure out which one was married to Uncle Jasper, Aunt Sarah would be the last one I'd pick. She always dressed up, even when she was just going to the grocery store. The only time I'd even seen her in her robe was the night her poodle "Prissy" got her head stuck between the banister posts and wouldn't stop howling.

2

Aunt Sarah was a big one for manners and etiquette and such. She was always fussing about using the correct fork, not eating with my elbows on the table and that kind of thing. It was hard to get mad at her though. Just when it seemed she'd wart you to death with her "don't do thats" and "mind your manners" she'd bake up a peach cobbler just for me and top it off with a big scoop of homemade vanilla ice cream, just to let me know she loved me.

Aunt Sarah was involved in all the social groups in St. John. Her weekly schedule included the Ladies Auxiliary, the Tea Society, the Garden Club, and any other group whose members were ladies with blue hair and who looked like they'd have a conniption fit if the gravy splashed onto their tablecloth during dinner.

The differences between Aunt Sarah and Uncle Jasper were probably best shown by their choice of canine companions. Aunt Sarah's dog, Prissy, was a registered toy poodle, constantly groomed and pampered. I bet Prissy had spent more time having her hair done than most of the women in St. John. I can't remember a time when the dog had gotten muddy, scratched at a flea, or even been forced to undergo the shame of not having all of her toenails freshly painted the same color. Prissy was so finicky she even refused to eat a piece of sausage or a wiener unless the casing was peeled off first.

In contrast, Uncle Jasper had Jake. Jake appeared to be a conglomeration of every breed known to man, but leaned mostly toward bloodhound. He was only given a bath once I know of, and that was in tomato juice after he had went a few rounds with a skunk, losing every one of them incidentally, that had taken up residence under our back porch.

Jake's favorite pastime was either lying on the porch in a stupor, so much so you had to push him out of the way with your foot to open the screen door, or noisily cleaning his manly parts with his tongue. This was one of the more pleasant surprises he could be counted on to provide at each and every one of the club meetings Aunt Sarah would host in her flower garden. On more than one occasion the ladies' tea was interrupted by the sight of Jake "locked up" in an amorous embrace with whichever bitch happened to be in heat at that time. I remember one particular occasion when the object of Jake's attempted lust was a Yorkshire Terrier owned by one of the other members of the Garden Club. Despite his best efforts the relationship was never consummated although if they'd ever made it to the back steps I imagine the Yorkie would have forever been ruined for others of her diminutive breed.

After that particular episode, which had ended in a frenzy of genital washing by Jake, Aunt Sarah had attempted to put her foot down.

"Jasper, I refuse to be embarrassed by that mongrel any longer. I want you to take him down to Doc West's this minute and get him fixed." Doc West was the only veterinarian in town and also owned a cafe out on the highway. As you might imagine, few of the locals ate there since the rumors about how he kept his prices so cheap began circulating.

Uncle Jasper was sitting in his recliner rolling one of his big cigars around in his mouth. He had taken to chewing on these since his wife and doctor had conspired to make him stop smoking. A good, fat one would last for nearly two hours before he had chewed and swallowed it down or before it got too slobbery to keep its shape.

He just looked at her over the top of the newspaper he'd been reading.

"If I'd wanted a girl dog, I'd have bought a girl dog," he said and turned the page.

That was the last word on the subject. Jake eventually died of old age, still a whole dog. To this day you can occasionally see one of his progeny

4

wandering around St. John, eagerly carrying on his grandfather's tradition.

The only thing Jake was good at, other than embarrassing Aunt Sarah, was finding me. When I was real little I tried to hide from my uncle and aunt a time or two, but all they had to do was turn Jake loose and he'd find me quicker than fried chicken disappeared from in front of a preacher at a Sunday dinner. I remember one time I tried to run away and got lost down in Good Hope bottom. Uncle Jasper finally found me by driving up and down the dirt roads until Jake caught a whiff of me and bailed out of the back of the pickup. I sure was glad to see him that night I'll guarantee you.

Anyway, as you can tell life around St. John, Texas was slow at best.

At least until me and Junebug Walker found the body.

# CHAPTER 2

It was right after school let out for the summer.

Me and Junebug rode our bikes down to Sandy Creek to see if we could catch a mess of catfish. We'd been there about an hour and still hadn't had a bite so Junebug decided to go swimming. I didn't waste any time shedding my clothes and jumping in after him. Even though the summer was already hot, the water was cold enough to take my breath away when I hit. That big rainstorm we'd gotten a couple of days before, the first in months, had raised the level of the creek and lowered the temperature.

I'd better tell you a little about my best friend, Junebug. Most people's first impression was that Junebug had something wrong with him. Not only was he scrawny for being twelve, but he also looked funny. When God was deciding on how to assemble Junebug Walker he must have either been having a bad day or was just plain mad at his parents.

Junebug was not only buck toothed to the point where he could eat a hamburger out of the bottom of a Mason jar, but was gotch-eyed to boot. I spent more time with him than anybody else on earth and I still couldn't tell which eye to look at when we were talking. I finally got in the habit of looking between his eyes at the top of his nose, since I figured that was kind of neutral ground.

Patches of his hair always stuck straight up, no matter how much time Mrs. Walker spent trying to make it behave. I remember one time when his momma sent him outside to play with so much styling gel on his hair that after it dried you could thump it and it'd hurt your finger. That experiment failed because by the time it set up an hour later he looked like a birds nest was attacking his head. Before it dried the hair dressing had apparently acted like a magnet and attracted every loose leaf and stick, along with a goodly amount of dirt, in their yard.

Like I said, most people thought Junebug was slow when they first met him, but they were bad wrong. Miss Bunion had given the class an I.Q. test the year before and he'd done so well she made him take it over just to make sure he hadn't cheated. After that she constantly rode him, saying anybody with his I.Q. could do better than B's and C's. It wasn't that Junebug wasn't smart enough to do well in his school work, he just wasn't interested.

What he was interested in was having fun and staying occupied. On this particular summer day we splashed around, took turns on the rope swing seeing who could go the farthest and make the biggest splash, and just generally having a good time. After a couple of hours of fooling around, Junebug's attention began to wander and suddenly I saw a twinkle in his gotch-eye.

"How many catfish do you think there are in this creek, Joe Ben?"

"I don't know. A bunch I'd imagine."

"Wouldn't a nice plate of fried catfish taste good?"

"Sure would."

"Fried catfish, fried potatoes, a couple of slices of Wonder bread and a big glass of your Aunt Sarah's iced tea. That's what I'd like."

"Umm hmmm," I agreed.

Junebug floated on his back for a few minutes in silence, then added, "Yup, nothing I like better than fresh, crispy catfish."

I began to get nervous, since it wasn't like Junebug to prattle without something in mind.

"Me too."

"I believe I'd do about anything for a couple of catfish to take home with us."

I didn't respond.

"What about you?" he asked as he began wading toward the bank.

"What about me what?"

"Wouldn't you be willing to do about anything for some fish?"

Now I was really worried. Junebug obviously had something in mind and wanted to feel me out before proposing it.

"Why?"

"Oh, I just heard about this new way to catch catfish. You like fishing don'cha?"

"Junebug, you know darn good and well I love fishing."

"Yeah, I thought so." He looked thoughtful for a moment. "How'd you like to learn a new way to fish?"

"What kind of new way?"

"Oh, just something I read about in a book the other day."

Junebug read more than any person I knew, except my Uncle Jasper. Every year he won the prize at the library given to the kid who read the most books over the summer.

He chose that moment to shut up and start skipping rocks across the creek. I waited until my curiosity couldn't take it any more.

"You know how much I hate it when you do that. What kind of new way to fish did you read about?"

"I don't want everybody to know about it else there won't be any fish left for us to catch."

"I won't tell anybody Junebug."

"Well, you really need two people to fish this way. If I tell you about it will you promise to help me?"

"Why don't you tell me about it first, then I can decide if I want to try it?"

"No, I'd better not. If you decide not to try it you might slip and tell somebody. If you're not interested I'll just get one of my other friends to help."

8

" Junebug, you know you don't have any other friends. Since you burned all the hair off of Denny Johnston nobody else's parents will let them play with you."

"If Denny had been paying attention it would have never blown up. Now do you want to help or not?"

I resigned myself to the inevitable since I knew Junebug was dying to try this sure fire fish catcher and wouldn't let me rest until he'd convinced me.

"All right, I promise I'll help. Now tell me how this works."

"It's really simple. The magazine said that during the summer the really big catfish get under rocks and logs and just lay there waiting for the creek to bring their food to them."

"So? I threw my bait close to every rock and log and didn't even get a nibble."

"That's why this system works so well, it doesn't matter whether the fish feel like eating or not."

"Junebug, my Aunt Sarah is nervous enough about me hanging around with you. I'm leaving if you're planning on using dynamite to blast them out."

"No, no, that's not it." He stopped for a minute and stared thoughtfully off into space, then frowned and shook his head. "Besides, I don't know anyplace we could get any dynamite. What we're gonna do is called 'noodlin'"

"Noodlin'?"

"Yeah. You find a nice hole, then reach under there and poke around till you feel ol' Mr. Catfish, then you grab him by the gills and flip him up on the bank. That's why you need two people, one to grab and flip and one to keep the fish from flopping back into the water."

I looked at him suspiciously. "Exactly which job did you have in mind for me?"

"Well, it would make more sense for me to stand up on the bank and watch so I can give you pointers and make sure you're doing it right."

"Nah. I think it'd make more sense for you to perfect the method first, and then tell me about it."

"Yeah, but you're taller so you could get into deeper water and get the bigger fish."

"Forget it. I'm not sticking my hand up under any logs until I see you do it a few times. If Denny had been more careful he wouldn't have to keep his head covered in suntan lotion all summer."

"All right, all right. I just thought you might want to be the one to tell everybody about how you just reached under a log and pulled out a big old catfish."

"That'd be a whole lot better than having to explain how I lost a couple of fingers when I grabbed a snapping turtle instead."

We argued back and forth for a while, but I was determined Junebug would be the first one to try a wild scheme of his for a change. Eventually he relented and gamely waded into the water, headed for a downed oak lying in the creek. I moved down the bank to where I would be in grabbing range if he actually managed to snatch a fish without getting his hand bit off.

He ducked his head and I could see mud churning up and discoloring the water as he frantically felt around on the muddy bottom. After a while he came up sputtering and spitting.

"Okay, your turn."

"No way. You obviously weren't doing it right so you need to keep practicing."

He muttered to himself but stayed in the water and moved further down the log. After a few deep breaths he disappeared under the surface again, but shot back to the top a second or so later.

"There's something up under here."

"What is it?"

10

"I don't know. It's too soft to be a turtle, but doesn't feel like a fish. Come out here and help me."

I took a few steps closer to the water, then stopped. "A snake'd feel pretty soft underwater wouldn't it?"

"I don't know, but whatever it is it's too big to be a snake. Now come on out here and quit being a sissy."

I wasn't going to let that sawed off runt call me a sissy and so waded out to where he was waiting.

"Let's both take a deep breath and go under. Reach under the log and grab hold, then brace your feet and pull hard."

I nodded and took three deep breaths, then ducked my head a second after I saw Junebug disappear.

The water in Sandy Creek was too murky to be able to see more than a few inches in front of my face. I felt my friend tap me then guide my arm up under the log.

I grabbed at the first thing I touched and yanked with all the strength I had in my twelve year old arms. Whatever the creek had lodged up under that old tree was stuck good, but I felt it beginning to give a little just as my breath ran out and I had to let go.

Junebug was gasping for air when my head broke the surface. "Nearly got it that time," he said.

"It sure felt funny, what do you think it is?"

"I don't know. Maybe it's one of those great big snakes like they have down in South America."

"Cut it out."

"Or maybe it's an alligator that's waiting for us to get him turned just right so he can grab us."

"If you keep on like that we'll never find out 'cause I'll get back on the bank."

There wasn't any stopping him once he got his imagination fired up and working.

"Or maybe it's one of those monsters like we saw on television last Saturday. You know, that one with the gills and claws and teeth. I'll bet that's exactly what it is...a monster that's been trapped up under there for years just waiting for two boys to come along and ..."

I didn't hear the rest of it. Just as he was working himself up to a feverish pitch the creek and log decided to let go of their catch. A blue tinged hand, followed by an arm covered in soggy clothing rose out of the water and began slowly falling toward Junebug.

I pointed behind him and started stuttering and stammering, trying to warn my best friend of his impending doom. He must have thought his narrative was scaring me because that too familiar gleam showed in his eye for the split second before the hand completed its plunge, ending up drooped across Junebug's shoulder and chest.

Even though I had a good three feet lead and longer legs he still beat me to the bicycles by a healthy margin, screaming all the while.

I never realized a bicycle could be pedaled fast enough to make the back tire spin but I swear that's exactly what happened. He didn't stop pedaling or screaming until we hit town, although I would have thought he had to take a breath sometime. I'm sure several of the little old blue haired ladies who did their shopping in the early afternoon got quite a shock at the sight of two boys pedaling their bicycles through town that fast, one shrieking like a banshee and both naked as jaybirds.

It was already shaping up to be an interesting summer.

# CHAPTER 3

By unspoken agreement, or maybe just because it was at the end of the street going into town, we'd headed directly to the sheriff's office and Uncle Jasper, busting in on him while he was shelling purple hull peas into a big tin wash pan.

"Sheriffyou'vegottacomequick..."

Junebug stopped for a moment, took a deep breath, and then started again.

"Wejustfoundadeadbodyoutatthecreekittriedtogr abmebutweranoffandcamehereandyou'vegottahurryitwa sunderalogbutweweretryingtoflipcatfishanditjustcameo utofthewaterand..."

"Junebug, stop your babbling. I can't hear myself think."

He reached into a bundle of laundry wrapped up on the floor next to him and calmly threw us two of his tee shirts, just as if having two naked boys screaming into his office was an everyday occurrence. Junebug's lower lip was quivering and he was hopping from foot to foot, too excited to stand still as he put his shirt on.

Uncle Jasper turned to me. "Joe Ben, can you tell me what happened?"

"Just like he said, we were down at Sandy Creek by the rope swing and a dead body came floating up and tried to grab Junebug."

"Are you sure it wasn't just somebody playing a trick on y'all? You know, trying to be funny."

"No, it was a dead body, all blue and slimy."

I saw Junebug shiver as he remembered the arm dropping down over him. "There wasn't anything funny about it."

My friend nodded his emphatic agreement.

13

"Well, I guess there isn't anything to do but go out there and have a look," Uncle Jasper grumbled as he put the pan of peas to the side.

"Cecil!" he hollered

"Yeah, Sheriff?" a voice from the back room responded.

"Get out here. We've got police work to do."

"Be right there."

A few seconds later Cecil waddled out of the back room, arms laden with wallpaper and speckles of glue dotting his uniform, silent testimony to his activities.

Uncle Jasper had been sheriff since the early fifties. Cecil Parker had hired on as his deputy right before I'd come to live with him and Aunt Sarah. Cecil weighed about two hundred and fifty pounds and was 5'8". In addition to being St. John's only deputy, Cecil was also a mechanic at Darrel's Gulf Station and incidentally, a distant cousin of ours although we generally didn't make that known.

"What's up?"

"These two," he motioned to us with his arm, "claim to have found a dead body down at the creek. We better check it out."

Cecil's eyes got real big. "A dead body! Wait just a minute."

He dropped his armload of wallpaper and returned to the back room at a trot, or at least what would have to pass for a trot. We could hear him rummaging around in the closet back there, eventually exclaiming in satisfaction as he apparently found the object of his search.

A few seconds later he came back to the front, dragging a mess of rubber and metal, sweating like a stuck pig and breathing heavy.

"This'll give us a chance to try out this underwater stuff I got from military surplus."

14

Now that he mentioned it I could tell the pile of stuff on the floor was one of those frogmen outfits like they showed James Bond using in the movies we'd seen at the theater. If they'd made that suit big enough to fit Cecil it must have used up enough rubber for a fleet of truck tires.

"Put that damn thing back up Cecil, else we'll be looking for two bodies in the creek. You don't no more know how to use that than I know how to fly a rocket ship. Now find your gun and badge and let's go."

Cecil hefted the pile of equipment and headed back toward the storage room, muttering low enough where we couldn't hear him. As he disappeared Uncle Jasper turned to us.

"Now you boys go on home and put some clothes on...and tell your Aunt Sarah I may be late for supper."

"But Sheriff, don't you need for us to go with you and show you where we saw the body?" Junebug asked.

"No. You and Joe Ben go to the house and get dressed. If I need to ask you anything I'll know where to find you."

Just then Cecil came out of the back room and they both went out the door. A moment later I heard the patrol car start and drive away.

**********************************

"Well, let's go," Junebug said after he'd dressed in some old clothes I loaned him.

"Go where?"

"To the creek, of course."

"Uncle Jasper told us not to come down there."

"No he didn't. He said for us to go home and get dressed and then he said he didn't need for us to show him where the body was. He never said we couldn't go down there and watch."

"I'm pretty sure that's what he meant."

15

"Let me ask you something Joe Ben...is your uncle a pretty smart fellow?"

"Sure."

"And has he ever been the least bit reluctant to tell you not to do something?"

"Well...no, not that I can remember."

"See there, if he didn't want you to come down there he'd have said so. I bet he just didn't want us down there messing up the crime scene until he got a chance to look at it."

"What crime scene?"

"The location of the murder of course. Joe Ben, sometimes you are so dense." He shook his head in apparent disgust.

"What are you talking about?"

"The body. Do you think that poor soul just put himself under that log?"

"Junebug, you get the wildest ideas of anybody I've ever seen or heard tell of."

"Maybe so, but I know a murder when I see one."

"When you see one? All you saw was that hand come down on your shoulder and then the bushes you passed through. I swear your feet didn't touch water or land from the creek to the road."

"Don't you go lying about me. I was just in a hurry to tell your Uncle Jasper about what we'd seen."

"You screamed like a girl all the way to town."

"That wasn't a scream, I was just...."

I could tell the wheels in his head were turning furiously in an attempt to come up with a halfway plausible explanation, at least to himself. After a minute it was clear his mental well had run dry.

"Joe Ben, you always change the subject when I'm winning an argument. We were talking about going down to the creek, now are you coming or not?"

I figured I knew what my uncle had meant, but the thought of seeing a real dead body was

16

overpowering. Of course, technically I'd already seen it, but the circumstances had removed any glamour from the moment although the excitement hadn't been diminished at all.

"All right, I'll go."

We climbed out the window and down the trellis so Aunt Sarah wouldn't have a chance to tell us not to go. I'd found that with Aunt Sarah it had always been more productive to ask forgiveness rather than permission.

The ride back to the creek took considerably longer than our ride into town had. I know it was probably my imagination, but I thought I occasionally caught a faint odor of scorched rubber left by Junebug's bicycle tires during his earlier retreat.

The patrol car was parked on the edge of the road to one side of the bridge. We dropped our bikes next to it and slid down the bank through the weeds, ignoring the briars that occasionally caught at our shorts.

Uncle Jasper and Cecil were out by the log poking under it with a couple of sticks. They obviously weren't having any luck and Uncle Jasper stopped and looked at us when we finished our slide and ended up on the creek bank.

"I thought I told you boys not to come out here."

"Sheriff, technically what you said was for us to go home and change clothes, you never actually told us not to....," Junebug stopped as Uncle Jasper waved at him.

"Forget it, I don't think I could bear to hear another one of your explanations."

He looked back to where Cecil was prodding around.

"Looks like you boys were imagining things. There isn't anything under that log but mud."

"But Uncle Jasper, it wasn't under the log when we left. We'd pulled it loose and it floated up right

17

there," I said pointing toward the middle of the eddy where Junebug had been standing. "Junebug, go stand right where you were".

He looked at me as if I'd just grown two heads.

"I believe he can tell where you're talking about. I've got a clean pair of shorts on and momma would kill me if I got 'em dirty."

I didn't know what he was so worried about. First of all, he was wearing a pair of my shorts and second, in all the time I've known Junebug I don't remember ever seeing him clean for longer than a couple of hours, and that was when we went to Sunday school and church.

Uncle Jasper leaned over and picked up a pine cone floating by and tossed it on the bank next to me.

"Throw this where the body was the last time you saw it."

I chunked it into the creek. "That's pretty close, maybe a foot to the right."

We stood there and watched the pine cone swirling around in circles for a few seconds. Eventually, the sluggish current carried it past the end of the log and back toward the middle of the creek.

"Come on Cecil," Uncle Jasper said as he began following the cone, careful to stay far enough back so he didn't affect its course.

Me and Junebug followed along on the bank, being careful to keep from slipping since the ground was still muddy from the rain. He stayed far enough away from the water to where he wouldn't be likely to fall in. Since I'd never known him to have an aversion to creek water, I guess being grabbed by a dead person had affected him more than he wanted to let on.

We followed the pine cone for a while as it meandered and wound its way down the channel. Uncle Jasper had always possessed an amazing ability to pick his way through the woods on our hunting trips, always managing to avoid stump holes, vines, and logs while never seeming to slow his steady pace. The same talent proved invaluable in this endeavor since he never got wet above the waist.

Cecil, however, fell every thirty feet. Uncle Jasper helped him up the first few times but eventually stopped, just looking disgusted when he heard the frequent splashes but not slowing in his pursuit of the pine cone.

Eventually we came around a bend to a jam of sticks, leaves and other flotsam, all held back by a tree which had apparently blown over in the last storm.

A few seconds later Uncle Jasper came around the curve and stopped, staring at the miniature logjam. We heard the sound of another splash, followed a minute later by Cecil half floating, half crawling down the creek, water running off of the beat up straw cowboy hat he wore.

"What'cha see?" Junebug hollered at Uncle Jasper from the top of the bank, which was about twenty feet up at this point.

Uncle Jasper just grunted and continued looking.

"Do you see anything?" he yelled again. I could tell from the sound of his voice he was excited again. I knew that if I turned around he'd be bouncing from foot to foot on the top of the bank like he was standing on hot coals.

"I said, do you see anyth....." Junebug's voice was abruptly cut off, immediately followed by a shower of dirt and gravel. A skinny form shot past me on its backside and sailed out over the creek, landing in the middle of the debris floating on the water.

He came up sputtering and coughing, face covered in leaves and bark from the pile-up. Before any of us had a chance to laugh that same blue tinged hand and arm rose out of the water once again and began its fall toward my friend.

19

\*\*\*\*\*\*\*\*\*\*\*\*\*\*\*\*\*\*\*\*\*\*\*\*\*\*\*\*\*\*\*\*\*\*\*

"You sure you're all right Junebug?" Uncle Jasper asked.

"Of course I'm all right, what makes you think I'm not?" He began looking around to be sure he wasn't bleeding from some unseen and unfelt wound.

"I've just never heard a boy scream like that. Shoot, when Chester Dorrance got his toe caught in the electric door at the Piggly Wiggly he didn't holler that loud. If I'd have been passing by on the road I'd have thought somebody was cutting a leg off of an eight year old girl."

Junebug just sat there and fumed. He'd been taught not to backtalk grown-ups, although if he could have thought of some explanation I imagine he'd have used it.

"Well, anyway...you found the body. Good work." He patted Junebug on the head and then stood and walked over to where Cecil was examining the corpse, which they'd dragged out onto a flat place on the bank.

I followed him, wanting to get a better look since I'd never seen a dead person who wasn't in a casket with flowers all around.

"Are you sure you want to look at this Joe Ben?" he asked, standing between me and the remains.

I nodded my head.

"A person that's drowned isn't a pretty sight."

I shrugged my shoulders.

"All right then, just be sure you don't mention this to your Aunt Sarah. I doubt she'd approve."

He stepped aside and allowed me to squat down for a better look.

The man was laid on his back. He was wearing a long sleeved plaid shirt, with the buttons partially undone from the bottom up. His trousers were the khaki work pants favored by many of the men who worked in

20

the steel mill down at Lone Star. One foot was covered by a tan slip-on boot, the other was bare.

His hair was black, with just a few streaks of gray. The face, although slightly bloated and blue, still looked kind of peaceful.

"Look at this," I said quietly to Junebug.

"Did you say something?"

I turned my head and saw Junebug still a good thirty feet away.

"Come look at this. Look's like something's been biting on him."

"Sure does." He didn't move any closer.

"Junebug, you can't see anything from back there."

"You shut up, I can see just fine."

Uncle Jasper said something to Cecil I couldn't quite hear, but which was followed by the deputy climbing up the bank to the road. I could hear his keys jingling and his shoes squishing as he headed toward the patrol car.

My uncle squatted down next to me and poked at the body with the eraser end of a pencil he carried in his pocket.

"You see how he's not very bloated? That means he's only been dead a little while."

"How do you know?"

"'Cause it takes a little while for the gases to start forming, but once they do a body swells up real fast," Junebug said.

We both turned to look at him again. He was about twenty feet away now, shifting from foot to foot.

"I read it in a Hardy Boys book a few months ago," he said sheepishly.

We turned our attention back to the cadaver.

"He's right, if he'd been dead very long he'd be a lot more swollen." He poked at some ragged places where the skin was torn. "Look here too. This is probably where turtles and some of the smaller fish

21

have been eating on him. As many snappers as there are in Sandy Creek, if he'd been in the water very long there'd be more damage."

"The 'gators would have probably got him too, huh Sheriff?" I could tell from his voice Junebug was getting closer.

Uncle Jasper shifted positions to the other side. "I don't see any bullet holes or knife wounds, he must have drowned. Funny, I haven't heard any reports of anybody missing." He took off his hat and scratched his head. "Damn, he sure looks familiar."

He reached down and began going through the corpse's pockets. After a moment he put a set of keys on the ground, a small pocketknife with some kind of bark showing around the blade, and a handful of change.

Unbuttoning the shirt pocket revealed a flat, rectangular case with a pair of those half glasses like Aunt Sarah used for reading inside, a pen, and a few scraps of water soaked paper.

Next, he reached up under the body and checked the right pocket, coming up empty. The left pocket contained a leather wallet. Uncle Jasper opened it up.

"Well, we know who he is now," he said looking at the driver's license.

"Who?" Junebug asked from right next to me.

"Theodore Duval. St. John's only claim to fame."

\*\*\*\*\*\*\*\*\*\*\*\*\*\*\*\*\*\*\*\*\*\*\*\*\*\*

Cecil came sliding back down the bank right about then, but managed to stop before he launched into the creek. He was lugging a big camera and a bag.

"I called them on the radio, Sheriff. The ambulance should be here any minute."

"You boys move back now. Let Cecil take his pictures. This is the first time he's had a chance to use

22

the camera since he went to the crime photography school two years ago."

Uncle Jasper and I moved to the edge of the creek where Junebug had made his slide.

"Who's Theodore Duval?" I asked.

"Ted Duval. He's that writer the society ladies always make such a big fuss over. He wrote a handful of books a few years ago that were bestsellers. Made quite a name for himself, though I haven't heard much about him lately." He paused for a minute. "Now that I think about it, I do remember Sarah prattling on about something to do with him last week."

Behind us we heard Cecil exclaim, "Junebug, quit poking at that body and get back. I'm trying to take o-fficial po-lice pictures here and I don't need some boy jabbing at the turtle bites with a stick."

"You know, it seems she was saying he'd come back to town to work on another book. I need to ask her about that as soon as we get back," Uncle Jasper continued.

"But what would somebody like that be doing out here in Sandy Creek?

"That's the million dollar question Joe Ben."

"Junebug, if you ruin one more of my pictures by getting your bony little body in front of me I swear I'll kick you right in your butt," Cecil hollered.

Uncle Jasper shook his head. "Those two make a pair don't they?"

"What are you gonna do now?"

"Now we wait until the ambulance gets here. They'll take the body over to Sumter and Doc Jackson will send it somewhere for an autopsy to find out what killed him. We'll go ahead and search the woods for a mile or so up from where you first saw the body and see if we can find any clues or anything unusual."

"Like what?"

"At this point, I don't really know. He obviously had to get here somehow so we'll look for his car, where he entered the water, that kind of thing. The most important point to remember in an investigation is to start with an open mind. That way you're more likely to be thorough. A lot of police decide what happened, then look for evidence to support that idea. The problem with doing things like that is you may miss an important clue which disproves that particular theory... and which may send an innocent man to prison."

Just at that moment we heard Cecil say, "Dagnamit, I told you to stay out of the way."

Both of us turned and saw Junebug bent over the body, poking at the hand which had twice grabbed him. Cecil drew back his foot, preparing to plant it in the seat of his britches. Unfortunately, the bank was muddy and Cecil's planted foot slipped when he put his weight on it and the big man tumbled into the creek with a splash, soaking a nearly dry Junebug once again.

"Cecil quit playing in the damn water, we've got work to do. Junebug, leave that poor man alone before he grabs you again," Uncle Jasper said, as I heard the ambulance stop on the roadway above.

Junebug leapt back and looked warily at the cadaver.

"Lord save me from idiots and twelve year old boys."

He adjusted the badge on his shirt and headed up the bank to show the ambulance attendants the best way down to the body.

# CHAPTER 4

"Scoop" Brown was a small, mousy looking man who always had the well chewed stub of a pencil stuck behind his ear and a little spiral notebook poking its ragged pages out of his pocket. The notebook seemed to have a never ending supply of pages because it looked like the same one Scoop had been carrying for years, whipping it out and scribbling furiously with the pencil stub each time anyone passed on a morsel he considered to be the least bit newsworthy.

Scoop was an excitable sort of fellow and had even run into the newspaper office one day screaming "stop the presses" at the top of his lungs, after witnessing a collision between one of Bubba Langdon's prize Red Angus bulls and a chicken truck. He should have known better since the St. John Jimplecute didn't even have any presses and had its weekly newspaper printed in another town.

His position as head reporter for the Jimplecute was due less to a degree in journalism and more to his having been born well. Doris Brown, his mother, not only owned the Jimplecute but also the local radio station which broadcast pre-recorded country and western programming 24 hours a day, save for the three hours a week during football season devoted to the St. John High School Fighting Pine Cones.

In addition to his duties as a reporter, Scoop also provided the play by play commentary for the Fighting Pine Cones' home games. Normally this would have posed no problem but Scoop had a tendency to stutter when he got excited, which he was prone to do at the football games. I could remember one time in a particularly close game, Larry Bob Benson had run 75 yards for the game winning touchdown. The parking lot was nearly empty by the time Scoop finally managed to spit out that the run, "involved p-p-p-p-p-particularly fine b-b-b-b-b-blocking by m-m-m-m-m-members of the P-p-p-p-p-pine C-c-c-c-cones freshmen c-c-c-c-class."

On this day he came running up to the sheriff's office while Uncle Jasper was still unloading our bikes from the trunk of the patrol car.

"Sheriff Jas-p-p-p-p-p-er, I heard you f-f-f-f-found somebody floating in the creek."

"Calm down, Scoop, calm down." He slammed the trunk and leaned the bikes against the building. "Actually, the boys here found the body, I just helped 'em fish it out of the water."

Scoop began scribbling furiously on his notebook with that stub of pencil.

"What happened Joe Ben?"

"We was out fishing and found him stuck under a log on Sandy Creek," Junebug said before I could respond.

"What condition was the body in when you found it?"

"Dead."

Scoop looked exasperated.

"Obviously it was dead, why else would it be in the water?"

"Well, we were in the water and we weren't dead."

The reporter took a rag out of his pocket and wiped his forehead.

"Let's try a different tact. Joe Ben," he looked at me directly, "how did y'all happen to find the body?"

Junebug started to interrupt again but Uncle Jasper clamped a hand across his mouth, cutting him off.

"We'd been out fishing and decided to swim for a while. Junebug was fooling around a log and felt

26

something underneath it. We went to yanking and it just popped out."

"What happened then?"

I started to tell him about Junebug's reaction but the look showing on my friend's face, at least that part I could see around my uncle's hand, indicated he would just as soon I not share this portion of our adventure.

"We rode back into town and got Uncle Jasper and Cecil."

"So I guess that'd explain the report of two boys streaking on their bicycles. It was really just you two in your swim suits."

"Well, it was probably us and we'd just come from swimming." I didn't bother to correct his erroneous assumption about our clothing.

Cecil opened the door to the office and we all followed him inside to the air conditioned comfort.

Uncle Jasper sat at his desk and Scoop sat down across from him.

"Sheriff, did you identify the body?"

"I believe I know who it is but you can't print it until I notify the family."

"Who?"

"Ted Duval."

"I'll be d-d-d-damned. I just talked to him a couple of days ago."

"What were you talking to him about?"

"We were going to do an article on him for the Jimplecute. You know, home town boy makes good."

"What'd he have to say?"

"He told me he was back in town working on a new book. Said it was sure to be a hit, something about a robbery."

"Another novel?"

"No, he said this one was non-fiction. Supposed to have been nearly finished. He was bragging about the huge advance he'd gotten from the publisher." Scoop looked envious as he relayed this piece of gossip.

"Where was he staying?"

"Over at Bessie Hardeman's place." Bessie ran an old fashioned boarding house.

"What do you know about him?"

"Not a lot. Was there any evidence of foul play?"

"Not that I could tell."

"Any idea how he died?"

"No, not right now. I'll know more after we've had an autopsy done."

Scoop closed his notebook and stuck the pencil stub back behind his ear. "I guess that'll do it for now. Will you holler at me if anything else develops?"

"Sure thing."

He turned toward us. "Come on Joe Ben, let's go see what Aunt Sarah cooked for dinner."

\*\*\*\*\*\*\*\*\*\*\*\*\*\*\*\*\*\*\*\*\*\*\*\*\*\*\*\*

"Ask them, y'all always have plenty."

"The amount of food isn't the problem."

"If you ask them I promise not to tell gross stories while we eat."

"No, Junebug. You know you give Uncle Jasper indigestion. He says every time you eat with us he has to have a bowl of Rolaids for dessert."

"He's just kidding. You know how much he likes me."

I raised my eyebrow and looked at him.

"Well, he's never told me he didn't like me so I give him the benefit of the doubt. I think he's just a little high strung."

"Why are you so set to eat here? Aunt Sarah made meat loaf and you know how nasty it is." Aunt Sarah was a great cook with two exceptions. She insisted on serving liver and onions at least once a week and she made the worst meat loaf in Baldwin County. She'd gotten the recipe from a friend of hers who had supposedly won an award at a cooking contest in Dallas

28

with it. I suspected Aunt Sarah had written the ingredients down wrong, but she insisted on serving it on a regular basis anyway. Even Jake wouldn't eat the leftovers.

He wrinkled his nose up. "I'll make do, we can always sneak a sandwich or something." He started wiggling and I could tell he was working himself into a tizzy.

"You know your uncle's gonna go back to the creek and search for clues this afternoon, we need to go with him and help."

"What do you know about searching for clues?"

"As much as you do. You walk around and keep an eye out for anything unusual."

"What makes you think he'll want our help?"

"Oh, he's too proud to ask for it, but I know he needs it. If we don't help who can he count on...Deputy Cecil?" He paused for a minute while I thought about this. "Joe Ben, this isn't a case where somebody stole a cow or a bicycle is missing, your uncle can use all the help he can get."

"You may be right, but how do we know he didn't just drown?"

"We don't, but why would a city slicker like that be out on Sandy Creek? He had all his clothes on so he wasn't swimming. I guess he might have been fishing, but I don't think so. No, I'd bet my reputation something funny's going on here."

"What reputation?"

"There you go again, changing the subject. I'm offering my services to help your uncle and you're being stubborn."

"All right, I don't suppose it'd hurt for us to just have a look. Four sets of eyes are better than two. Let's go downstairs and ask Uncle Jasper."

"Are you crazy? If we ask him he'll just say no. Let's just wait here till he leaves and then follow him out there on our bikes."

"How do you know he won't come up here and tell us to stay home?"

"Joe Ben, sometimes you just don't think. If you didn't want me to go somewhere with you, would you tell me you were leaving or try and slip out unnoticed?"

He had a good point. Nothing made Junebug more determined than to have somebody tell him he couldn't do something.

While we waited for the coast to clear he dug around in my closet, eventually pulling out an old Kodak camera Aunt Sarah had given me for Christmas two years ago and a magnifying glass with a cracked lens we'd found in a trash barrel.

"These might come in handy." He stuck the magnifying glass into his front pocket and hung the camera around his neck by the strap.

"Now we need a plan."

"What in the world do we need a plan for, Junebug? All we're gonna do is pedal out to the creek and look around the woods."

"That's your problem Joe Ben, you don't think things through."

"I don't think things through? That's the pot calling the kettle black. Who's the one that nearly gave old Widow Clements a heart attack when she saw the armadillo somebody'd dipped in glow in the dark paint and covered in feathers?"

"How was I to know church would let out late that night? Besides, I was trying to scare her dog, not her, so that doesn't count."

He clammed up and sat there looking put upon until we heard the front door close followed shortly by the sound of Uncle Jasper's patrol car starting up and pulling away. We waited a while then headed out my window again, Junebug nearly strangling himself when the camera strap got caught on the window latch.

We'd nearly made it to the ground when we were startled by a voice behind us.

"Looks like I'm gonna have to either nail that window shut or move the trellis before y'all kill all of Sarah's roses."

"Darn it Sheriff, you're gonna scare somebody to death sneaking up on 'em like that. Especially somebody that's been through everything we have today," Junebug said as he jumped the last few feet.

"Sarah catches you stomping all over her flowers and you'll be lucky if all she does is scare you. What are y'all up to anyway?"

"Uh..uh..uh," Junebug stuttered as he tried to come up with a convincing story. Being grabbed by a dead man must have been a trying experience since he wasn't as quick in concocting stories as usual.

"Don't bother with one of your fabrications," Uncle Jasper said. "I was just wondering if y'all were interested in helping me search for clues back at the creek?"

"Do you mean it?" I asked.

"Yup."

Junebug looked at him suspiciously. "Why do you want us to come with you?"

"Let's just say I heard somewhere that four sets of eyes were better than two."

Me and Junebug looked at each other. Surely Uncle Jasper couldn't have heard what we'd been saying.

"Besides, if I've got you two in sight I know you're not tromping around destroying evidence." He looked thoughtful for a second. "Maybe I'd better make Cecil stay close too."

\*\*\*\*\*\*\*\*\*\*\*\*\*\*\*\*\*\*\*\*\*\*

It was nearly four o'clock before we made it back to Sandy Creek. We decided to start from where we'd first seen the body and spread out about twenty feet apart in a line to comb the woods. Uncle Jasper was nearest the creek, then Junebug, me and Cecil.

31

"That way we've got somebody with sense next to the one without." From the way he said it I believe he was lumping Junebug and Cecil in the same group.

We covered nearly a mile before Uncle Jasper yelled for us to stop, then motioned to come over to him.

He was looking into a little clearing by the creek, an old fashioned bicycle leaning against a tree and a lawn chair and an assortment of items scattered around.

"Cecil, take some pictures."

The deputy began clicking away from various angles. Within a moment Junebug was doing the same, usually from right in front of whatever Cecil was trying to photograph.

Uncle Jasper was staring intently at the site, as if trying to freeze a mental image.

"Sheriff, can't you get him out of the way?" Cecil asked in exasperation.

Without taking his eyes off of the objects, Uncle Jasper leaned over and picked Junebug up by the scruff of his neck, absent mindedly putting him down next to me.

"Be sure and get pictures of that path leading down to the creek...and save a few exposures in case we need them."

Junebug pointed the camera at a section of the ground that looked as if it had been swept clean and clicked a few times.

I moved to where I could get a better look at the area now that Cecil had finished his work.

A folding lawn chair was lying on its side not far from the creek. A yellow pad covered in writing was on the ground next to the chair, not far from the remains of a half eaten sandwich crawling with ants. A soda can was overturned not far from the sandwich.

Without saying a word Uncle Jasper stood and began walking toward the creek, careful to stay several feet away from the strange looking path. Junebug and I followed quietly, emulating my uncle's slow walk and meticulous examination of the area.

The creek bank didn't reveal anything unusual, although we spent a long time examining the place where the path entered the water. There was one partial footprint and what appeared to be marks left by fingers right at the edge of the water, although most of it appeared to have been swept away, as if by a broom.

"Hmmph," Uncle Jasper grunted, then began looking along the creek. Eventually he stopped and then without warning, jumped into the creek, clothes and all.

"Go on Junebug, jump in," I urged.

He looked at me like I was nuts, shaking his head emphatically. I guess being grabbed by a corpse twice in one day had soured him on the notion of swimming in Sandy Creek for a while.

"Both you boys stay up there. I'll just be a minute."

He grabbed a branch covered in leaves that was caught against a log and swam back over to where we were waiting. Grabbing a root, he pulled himself out of the water.

"Look here." He held the branch out for us to see.

The leaves were still mostly green, although wilted. Fresh wood showed at the bottom where it'd been cleanly cut.

Uncle Jasper walked back to where Cecil was waiting, using his handkerchief to carefully place the various items around the lawn chair into plastic bags. We tagged along again, Junebug being uncharacteristically quiet.

"It was a tuna fish sandwich Sheriff. I managed to brush all the ants off before I bagged it."

"Good work Cecil." He rolled his eyes at me.

"What are you so quiet about Junebug?" Uncle Jasper asked.

"I'm just thinking."
"God help us all."

# CHAPTER 5

Bessie Hardeman ran the closest thing to a hotel that St. John had available. Her two story boarding house could accommodate nine guests, although the most she'd ever had was six, and that was when the oil boom had been roaring down around Kilgore. The boom here had faded to a whisper when it was determined Baldwin County appeared to be one of the few in this part of the country which had managed to avoid having oil and gas underneath it.

Rumor had it Mr. Hardeman had been a moonshiner, making white lightning and selling it in the dry counties that virtually covered East Texas. He'd died a few years before Uncle Jasper had taken office and any money Bessie Hardeman had nowadays came from boarding guests or the meals she served at lunchtime in a little diner down the road from her house.

We'd gotten home right at dark the day before, so Uncle Jasper had put off searching Ted Duval's room until the next day. We walked out of the house bright and early to find Junebug sitting on the hood of the patrol car waiting on us. Uncle Jasper didn't reply to his cheerful "Good morning", just motioned for us to get in the car.

As it turned out, getting a look at the room required some persuading on Uncle Jasper's part.

"Now Bessie, I'm the sheriff and I can look in his room if I want to."

"I watch Dragnet. I know you have to have a search warrant."

"That's only if we're looking for evidence of a crime. I'm trying to find out where I can contact his next of kin."

"I still don't like the idea of you snooping around one of my guest's rooms without their permission."

"Your guest is dead, I'm pretty sure he won't be complaining."

"What are you looking for?"

"I can't discuss that with you Bessie, now are you gonna let me have a look around or should I go ahead and arrest you for obstructing justice?"

"You wouldn't dare!"

"I might."

They stared at each other in silence for a minute before she finally relented.

"All right, you win. Let me go get my....Junebug Walker, you put that down. That came all the way from Los Angeles, California."

He quickly replaced the crystal bell he had been examining on the table.

"Mind you don't touch anything else. Jasper, you keep their grubby little hands off of my things while I look for the key."

She disappeared through the doorway leading into her dining room.

"She's just mad because she didn't get a chance to plunder through his things first," Uncle Jasper whispered to me.

She returned a few minutes later carrying a ring of keys.

"Come on, I haven't got all day."

We followed her up the stairs and down the hall. She stopped in front of a door and picked through the keys, finally choosing one and inserting it in the lock.

"Does anyone else have a key to this room?" Uncle Jasper asked her.

"No, I keep the only set. If the guests want to get in they have to come ask me."

Uncle Jasper looked at us. "Y'all don't touch anything inside or even enter the room. Cecil has to come over and take pictures before we disturb anything, just in case."

The door swung open and Uncle Jasper took a step forward, stopping suddenly. This caused Junebug, who had been right behind him, to run into his legs and bounce back.

From what I could see around my uncle someone had already been in the room. There were clothes scattered everywhere, the bed and night table were overturned, and papers blew this way and that with each gust of wind coming through the open window.

\*\*\*\*\*\*\*\*\*\*\*\*\*\*\*\*\*\*\*\*\*\*\*\*\*\*

Cecil came right over and took more pictures, Junebug on his heels with my Kodak. It looked like the Baldwin County Sheriff's Office was finally getting their money's worth out of the camera equipment.

After he finished and went outside, Uncle Jake entered the room and began carefully picking up items and examining them.

He'd told us, "Boys, y'all be sure and don't touch anything. If you notice something suspicious tell me and I'll look at it with you." He looked us directly in the eyes. "And I'm not joking about this. If you really want to help that's fine, but you can ruin a perfectly good piece of evidence by touching it if you're not properly trained. Do you both promise?"

We nodded our heads emphatically.

"All right then, be careful. And don't kneel or sit on the floor, the carpet's soaking wet."

The pillows had been cut open and were now soggy masses of feathers under the window. A typewriter lay on the floor amidst them. Sodden papers, some containing typewriting, some handwritten, some blank, were scattered on the side of the room nearest the window, while others blew back and forth. Uncle Jasper squished his way across the carpet and shut the window.

An hour later a list had been made of everything in the room. Uncle Jasper would identify something as he examined it and I would dutifully make a note of its name. Junebug quickly tired of this and went outside to take pictures of the window and grounds.

"This must be the introduction to that book he was working on," Uncle Jasper said as he examined one of the dry pages.

It was titled "The Great East Texas Bank Robbery" and the text began midway down the page. I read while he continued looking;

> "It was a cold winter day in 1952 when three armed men entered the Farmer's Savings and Loan in St. John, Texas. Within minutes the masked men had locked the doors and moved all of the employees and clients into the vault. Two satchels were quickly filled with currency while a third was used to hold the contents of the safety deposit boxes.
>
> The robbery was almost complete when the seventy year old security guard, Wendall Hobbs, made a movement which was apparently interpreted by one of the robbers as reaching for his revolver. Shots were fired and after the blue smoke of the gunpowder cleared, seventy one year old Wendall Hobbs and four other innocent victims lay dead or dying in a pool of their own blood, unfortunate casualties of gunfire and ricochets.
>
> The crook's abandoned car was located the next day near Sandy Creek on the outskirts of town, but no sign of the criminals was ever discovered and their identity remains a secret...until now.
>
> I was raised in St. John and remember the excitement generated by this event. This book is

about the attempts of a humble mystery writer to solve a mystery from his childhood. In my quest I discovered the true identity of these bloodthirsty bandits and reveal it for the first time in this book."

That was where the page ended.

"Uncle Jasper, do you see page two of this?"

"Nope, sure don't. That appears to be the only page of the book that's here. I do see a letter from the publisher about it though. Looks like they were expecting delivery in the next couple of weeks. He must have been almost finished."

He stacked all of the dry papers into one pile and all of the wet ones into another.

"Let's take these with us, might be something in there."

"When can I clean this mess?" Bessie asked as we started down the stairs carrying our papers.

"In just a minute, I need to ask you a few questions first."

About that time Junebug came wandering back in the door.

"All finished, Chief," he said flipping a two fingered salute at Uncle Jasper.

"Don't call me chief. You and Joe Ben sit down right over here and stay quiet." He sat on the couch and motioned for Bessie Hardeman to sit in a chair in front of him. After she did so he continued.

"Has anybody else entered that room since Mr. Duval left?"

"Not through the door, they'd have had to come in through the window."

"What about the window? Do you know why it would have been left unlatched?"

"Oh, that latch hasn't worked in years. If you want to open it all you have to do is push up."

"How long had Mr. Duval been renting a room from you?"

"A little over two weeks."

"What kind of a tenant was he?"

"Good. Never made much noise, didn't ask me to cook anything special. Pretty much stayed in his room and kept to himself."

"Did he have any visitors?"

"A few. Scoop Brown came by last week, then some woman was over here the same day Mr. Duval disappeared, that's all I can think of."

"What did this woman look like?"

"Looked like a city woman. Wearing one of them short skirts, blonde out of a bottle hair, boots up to the knees, lots of makeup. She was driving a blue convertible and crying when she left."

"Do you know who she was or what she was crying about?"

"Nope. He didn't mention and I didn't ask. Sometimes people ask too dang many questions." She looked pointedly at him when she said this.

He ignored her comment.

"When was the last time you saw him?"

"It would have been three days ago now. He left on his bicycle right before that big thunderstorm started. I remember because it was clouding up and looked like rain so I asked him if he needed to take an umbrella with him and he just ignored me."

"Did anything unusual happen?"

"Not that I remember."

"How long did he have that room rented for?"

"His rent was up the same day he left."

"Why didn't you call us when he didn't show back up?"

"I didn't think it was necessary. He'd taken off for a few days before without saying anything."

Uncle Jasper stood up. "All right Bessie, that's all I can think of right now. If anybody else shows up you be sure and send them over to see me. In the meantime you can dry your carpet but lock the room, don't take anything out, don't let anybody else into it without my permission."

"But what if somebody wants to rent it?"

"Bessie, you've got nine rooms. How many boarders do you have right now?"

"None, but you never know."

"I'll tell you what, if you suddenly have a busload of tourists show up to rent rooms, you call me and I'll come right over and clean that one out. Otherwise, you don't let anybody in there." He turned to leave, then stopped and looked back at her.

"And don't you go digging through that stuff neither. You find something else to gossip about other than that poor man's belongings."

\*\*\*\*\*\*\*\*\*\*\*\*\*\*\*\*\*\*\*\*\*\*\*\*\*\*

Junebug apparently decided Uncle Jasper could handle things by himself for a while.

"Let's take this film down to the drug store and get it developed," he said when he pedaled up to my house after lunch. I had been in the front yard unsuccessfully trying to convince Jake to fetch a stick.

"All right, let me go tell Aunt Sarah where we're going."

"Aunt Sarah," I yelled as I went through the front door.

"In the kitchen," she answered.

She was standing at the counter peeling apples to fill the pie crusts in the pan next to her. "I'm going to the drug store with Junebug, all right?" I asked.

"Don't let that boy talk you into doing anything you shouldn't. Remember poor Denny Johnston."

That seemed to be the refrain used by most parents in town when asked by their children if they could play with Junebug. Remember poor Denny Johnston. I sometimes wonder if that's what Mrs. Walker told Junebug's little brother when they played together.

"I'll use my head."

"Here," she said reaching for her purse. "You and Junebug get some ice cream while you're there." That's what I loved about Aunt Sarah. One minute she's worrying you to death and the next she's buying you ice cream.

"Thanks. We'll be back in a little while."

We parked our bikes in front of Gleason's Drug Store and entered the air conditioned paradise. The pharmacy was in the back of the store, in the front was the lunch counter, a magazine and comic book rack, cosmetic counter, and an assortment of other merchandise to be inspected and purchased while waiting for a prescription to be filled.

We went to the counter and handed three rolls of film to Miss Polly. She had one of those beehive hairdos and always wore a set of glasses on a chain around her neck although I don't recollect ever seeing her actually wearing them.

"Ask them to be extra careful with these. They're official police photographs," Junebug said.

"Is that right? Did your uncle send these over Joe Ben?"

"No, they're ours," I answered.

"I thought they were police business."

"They are, we're helping Sheriff Jasper with his investigation." Junebug's scrawny chest swelled up with self importance.

"Isn't that cute?" I could tell that remark deflated him a little. "You're just the sweetest little things, pretending to help the sheriff." She took the rolls of film and started filling out a form.

"What kind of crime are you investigating?" She said this in a tone of voice like she was asking two little girls playing in the mud what kind of pies they were making.

Junebug got that twinkle in his eye again.

"A murder."

42

Miss Polly looked up. "A murder! My lands, who's been murdered?"

I casually kicked Junebug on the side of the leg. He ignored me.

"Ted Duval. We found his body floating in the creek, all blue and swole up and putrefied. The turtles had been eating on him and...OW! Joe Ben quit kicking me."

Miss Polly was looking a little green around the gills.

"When will the film be back?" I asked her while Junebug furiously rubbed on his leg where I'd kicked him the second time.

"Should be a couple of days. Why don't you boys run along and play now?" Apparently she'd had enough of conversing with Junebug.

I shrugged my shoulders and headed to the lunch counter, stopping briefly to pick up a comic book from the rack. Junebug did the same, limping along beside me. We were soon licking on chocolate ice cream cones and lost in the world of super heroes.

Superman was just getting ready to put a whipping on Lex Luthor when Junebug leaned over and interrupted. "Joe Ben, look." He motioned with his head toward the back of the store.

A blonde woman entered the rear door and walked to the cosmetic counter. She was wearing hot pants and go-go boots like those women on "Laugh-In". I wasn't supposed to watch that show but had occasionally caught an episode when Aunt Sarah wasn't home.

"Let's go see what kind of car she's in." I headed for the back door.

We edged out the rear entrance and looked over the parking lot shared by the drug store, the Dollar General, and two or three other shops. In the parking space closest to us was a shiny, blue Corvette convertible.

43

We broke into a run, headed to the sheriff's office, dodging cars and causing several of the drivers to let out a stream of profanity which would have caused Junebug to blush, if we'd had enough time to think about it.

Without the adrenaline provided by sheer terror I beat Junebug to the office by a good ten feet and threw the door open, barely slowing as I passed through.

Cecil had apparently been asleep with his feet up on the desk. When the door busted open, he instinctively tried to propel himself out of his chair, unfortunately forgetting to take his feet off the desk first and only succeeding in pushing the chair out from under him, landing flat on his back behind the desk.

"Gosh Cecil, what'cha doing?" Junebug asked as he peered around the desk at the fat deputy, who looked remarkably like a turtle stranded on his back as he tried to get up.

"What in tarnation are you boys so excited about this time?" he asked as he struggled to his feet, ignoring Junebug.

"Where's Uncle Jasper?" I asked.

"He went down the block to get a haircut, I expect he'll be back any minute."

"Can't wait, no time." With that, Junebug was out the door at a dead run with me following two steps back.

Lester Thomas owned the only barber shop in town, located next to the Dollar General store. I could see Uncle Jasper sitting in one of the chairs talking to some of the other old timers spread out across the shop.

The talk stopped as we ran through the door with Junebug yelling, "Sheriff, come quick we found her."

"What?"

44

"The blonde lady, Sheriff, the blonde lady. We found her at the drug store."

"Joe Ben, what's he babbling about this time?"

"We were over at the drug store when this woman came in, looked just like the one Miss Hardeman was saying come to see Mr. Duval. She even had a blue convertible, just like she said."

"Well why didn't y'all say so? Lester, I'll be back later. I've got some sheriffing to do."

We headed out the door again at a run, Uncle Jasper following at a quicker than normal pace.

As Junebug and I rounded the corner into the drug store's parking lot, I saw the lady coming out of the rear entrance, walking toward her car. Junebug put on a burst of speed and passed me.

Just as the woman opened the door of her car he yelled out, "Stop in the name of the law! You're under arrest!"

She took off her sunglasses and watched us run across the asphalt toward her, obviously unsure as to what to do. I assume she wasn't used to having four and a half feet tall, gotch-eyed deputies screaming at her while they were running across a parking lot.

Uncle Jasper came around the corner just about the time Junebug launched himself and grabbed the woman around the legs.

She stumbled backwards but managed to keep from falling, despite the imp wrapped around her lower legs. After she regained her balance she just stood there, occasionally shaking a leg to try and loosen his grip, until Uncle Jasper arrived.

"Boy, have you lost what little mind you had?" He reached down and pried Junebug's arms from around her legs. "I'm sorry ma'am, I guess the heat got to him."

"You sure have young deputies in these parts Sheriff. Enthusiastic, but young." She brushed herself

45

off. "Did I understand him correctly? Am I under arrest?"

"No ma'am. Someone told us that a woman matching your description visited Ted Duval a few days ago and I need to talk to her."

"That would be me Sheriff. I hope that lovely landlady was flattering in her depiction of me." Obviously the woman knew who had blown the whistle on her.

"I can truly say she didn't do you justice."

All this beating around the bush and sweet talk was getting old quick. Apparently Junebug thought so too.

"What can you tell us about a man named Ted Duval?" he asked.

She turned her attention, and a pair of eyes as blue as the water in the town swimming pool, to him then held out her hand. Junebug, after looking to be sure his was clean, shook it.

"I'm Junebug Walker."

"Well, Deputy Junebug. I imagine I can tell you anything you need to know about Ted. My name is Julia. Julia Duval. I'm his wife."

# CHAPTER 6

"His wife?" Uncle Jasper asked.

"That's right. You sound surprised, didn't Ted mention he was married?"

"Actually ma'am, I've never talked to Mr. Duval."

"Is he in some kind of trouble? Is that why you were looking for me?"

Uncle Jasper took off his straw hat and held it by the brim with both hands, turning it nervously.

"Ma'am I really don't know quite how to tell you this so I'll just do it right out. We have reason to believe your husband may be dead."

She raised her hands and placed them on each side of her nose, cupping them to cover her mouth for a moment before lowering them again then leaning against her car for support.

"Oh no. How did it happen?"

"We're not sure yet. My nephew Joe Ben and Junebug here," he motioned toward us, "found a body floating in the creek yesterday. I recognized him from his picture in the paper."

"This is so terrible. Ted was such a good man."

"We may need you to make a positive identification of the body, after the coroner is through of course."

As she shook her head affirmatively, I could see tears in the corners of her eyes. I guess Junebug could too because he remained quiet.

"Would you mind if I ask you a few questions, or would you rather wait until later?"

"No, go ahead. I'll be fine."

"How long were you and Mr. Duval married?"

47

"About eight years, but to be honest, we've been separated for the last three."

"Separated?"

"Yes. Neither one of wanted to be the one to file for divorce, but we haven't lived together for three years. We were good friends, but terrible spouses."

"What was he doing in St. John?"

"You know he was born here?"

Uncle Jasper nodded his head.

"He wrote his first two novels before he graduated from high school, but didn't publish them for years. Not only were they his first two, they were also his best. He had an idea for a book that he'd been researching for the past couple of years, but wanted to come back here to write it. I think he hoped it would be good luck. A lot of writers are like that."

"What do you mean?"

"Superstitious. Some only write at a certain time of the day, some use the same typewriter, that kind of thing. Ted always insisted on using the same pen and refused to write on anything but those yellow legal pads. He also refused to start typing until he was completely finished with his writing."

"Anything else?"

"Yes, he liked to write outdoors. Most writers prefer working in an office but Ted always tried to get away by himself in the woods to do his writing. He said it was easier to concentrate there."

"Bessie Hardeman said she saw you come visit him right before he disappeared. What was that about?"

"Like I told you, we were still good friends. Ted just wasn't meant to be married. I still visit him regularly and we made it a point to go out to eat at least once a week."

"What did y'all do that day?"

"We just talked for a while, then he told me he was going to do some more writing that day and asked if I'd run over here to the drug store and get him a tuna fish sandwich to take with him."

"Did you?"

"Yes, sure did. I took it back to him, we talked for a little while longer then I left."

"Do you know what his new book was going to be about?"

"He said it had something to do with a bank robbery y'all had here back in the fifties. He wouldn't tell me too much, he said it was too dangerous."

"What did he mean by too dangerous?"

"I don't know. He acted really funny about this book, like he didn't want anybody to know anything about it. I know he already had a publishing contract for it once it was finished."

"Do you know if he had any enemies?"

"Ted? Probably. He wasn't the easiest person to get along with. He tended to see things from one point of view...his."

"Anybody in particular?"

"No, not that I can think of." She grasped Uncle Jasper by the forearm. "Why? Do you think there was foul play involved?"

"It's too early to know for sure, I just want to make sure I cover all the bases. What are you doing in St. John today?"

She appeared to be at a loss for a moment and Junebug took this opportunity to begin inspecting the sports car, looking at the mag wheels, the hood, and eventually into the driver's compartment.

"I...was coming down to see if Ted wanted to have lunch. I'm staying with a friend down in Tyler for a few weeks."

"Where do you usually live?"

"In Houston, not far from Ted's house."

"Are you planning to go back there anytime soon?"

"No, I hadn't planned to. Maybe I'd better stay here in case you need anything else...and somebody will need to make the arrangements for Ted's funeral."

"That's true, it might not be a bad idea for you to stick around. Bessie Hardeman is kind of cantankerous but she keeps a neat house and is one of the best cooks you'll find anywhere."

"Thanks, I'll see if she has a room open."

"She always does." He took a step and grabbed Junebug, who was leaned over inside the car so far his feet were off the ground and kicking.

"Why don't you go on over and rest up a bit? If I need you I'll know where to find you."

"I think I'll do that. I need some time to myself," she said as she opened the door and climbed into the car. The car cranked with the roar of the powerful engine underneath its hood.

"Oh, Mrs. Duval. One more question."

She stopped revving the engine and allowed the car to settle into a muffled rumble as it idled.

"Yes?"

"I need to notify Mr. Duval's other relatives, how do I get in touch with them?"

"You can't, I'm the only family he has left."

"His sole heir?"

"I hadn't thought of that but I suppose you're correct."

Uncle Jasper stepped back out of the way of the car and she pulled off, squealing the tires slightly as she turned onto the street.

"She seemed like a nice lady," I said to Junebug as my uncle walked back in the direction of the barber shop.

"Is that right? Then answer this; if she was just coming over here to visit for a couple of hours why was there a suitcase in the passenger's seat? And why was there a black funeral dress laid carefully on top of it?

That's not something I'd expect somebody who dressed like her to carry around with them."

**************************

Mr. Duval's funeral, held about a week after we talked with his wife, was well attended. Most of St. John's residents turned out to pay their last respects to its most famous son, although he probably wouldn't have been recognized by most people in town.

Mrs. Duval sat on the front pew of the church, and in one of the few chairs at the graveside service. She wore her black dress Junebug had seen in the car and a black hat with a veil covering her face. She cried a little, but nothing like the histrionics we saw at a lot of the funerals.

Me and Junebug were both wearing suits, although his showed a goodly portion of his ankles due to a growth spurt he was experiencing. Mrs. Walker had even managed to get most of his hair to lie down, although she still occasionally had to lick her fingers and swipe them across the top of his head as a cowlick started sprouting its way toward the roof.

Uncle Jasper and Aunt Sarah had me and Junebug sitting between them and Mrs. Walker. Although we both fidgeted in the heat, neither of us talked much during the service, out of respect for poor Mr. Duval. We did manage to start a good game of thumb wrestling before Mrs. Walker popped her son on the back of the head. The only other diversion from the long winded preacher was when Junebug pulled up his pants leg and picked at a scab until he got it bleeding real good. Another pop and a quick wipe with one of his mom's tissues removed this last bit of entertainment.

Afterwards, as people lined up to walk past the closed casket Junebug made a beeline for the back door. I guess he wasn't a hundred percent sure Mr. Duval wouldn't try to make one final grab at him.

51

After the graveside service, while the adults stood around and talked, we made our way back to the church steps and sat down in the shade.

"What'd the doctor who examined the body tell your Uncle Jasper?"

"Nothing yet, he had to send some samples to a lab in Dallas for tests."

"They still don't know what killed him?"

"Nope. I heard Uncle Jasper tell Cecil it'd probably be awhile before they knew anything."

I noticed Junebug looking over in the direction of a group of adults I didn't recognize.

"What'cha looking at?"

"Oh, nothing."

Eventually I caught a flash of blonde hair, and a girl peeked around the edge of a man's leg.

"Who's that?" I asked.

"I don't know, I've never seen her before."

I kept a watch on the little girl out of the corner of my eye.

"Are you sure you don't know her? She sure is looking at you a lot."

"Darn it Joe Ben, I said I don't know her. Carolyn Jenkins is supposed to have a cousin coming to stay with her for a while, maybe that's who she is."

"That's Carolyn's daddy there. I bet you're right. But why does she keep looking at you?"

"Beats me. Is there something wrong with the way I look?"

"No more than normal, although you're not usually this clean."

"Quit joking around, you know what I meant."

Just at that moment Carolyn Jenkins ran up to the group and took the new little girl by the hand and pulled her off to the side. The two of them stood there whispering and giggling for a second, then started walking toward us.

Carolyn and I had had a torrid romance for a couple of days in the spring. It ended when I found out she was allergic to dogs and didn't like to fish. I still thought she was cute and a lot of fun to hang around with...for a girl.

"Hi Joe Ben, hi Junebug," Carolyn said as they walked up. She fluttered her eyelashes at me. Aunt Sarah said it was cute but I always thought it made her look like she had something in her eye.

"Hi Carolyn," I said. Junebug just raised his hand in greeting.

"I wanted to bring my cousin over to meet y'all. She'll be staying with us for the next couple of weeks." The other little girl was busy examining her shoes and shifting from foot to foot.

"Joe Ben, Junebug, this is my cousin Danielle. Danielle, Joe Ben and Junebug."

Danielle looked up and into Junebug's eyes, ignoring me. I heard Junebug swallow loudly as I stared at her. Danielle's right eye looked straight ahead while her left tended to wander to the side. She was the first gotch-eyed girl I'd ever seen. Her and Junebug made a perfect pair.

He elbowed me in the ribs to stop my staring.

"Nice to meet'cha Danielle," I said remembering my manners.

"Howdy," Junebug mumbled. Now he was staring at his feet as she was staring at him.

"Pleased to meet you. Carolyn has told me so much about you two."

"She has?" Junebug asked suspiciously. "Like what?"

"Like how you two were the ones who found the dead man and how you even went into the water to help drag him out."

"Well, that's not exactly how it happened. You see, Junebug was standing at the top of the bank and it

53

was real muddy..." I stopped as his bony elbow buried itself between two of my ribs again.

"Yup, we were right there the whole time. We're even helping Sheriff Jasper conduct his investigation."

"Really? That's so exciting!"

"I reckon he couldn't do it without us."

Junebug's scrawny chest swelled up as he told Danielle all the details, starting with our trip to the creek and ending with the funeral that day. To hear him tell it you'd think he'd let me and Uncle Jasper tag along because he was too young to drive. He was also a lot braver in his version than I remembered.

"Junebug, I didn't hear you mention what happened when his arm dropped across you."

"Hush Joe Ben, I'm telling this story."

"Are you about ready? I was thinking about going fishing down at the pond today."

"Nah, I believe I'll stay awhile and talk to Carolyn and Danielle." He looked at them. "That is, unless y'all are fixing to leave."

"No, we'd love to hear you tell us some more about the investigation, wouldn't we?" Carolyn looked at Danielle, who giggled and smiled at Junebug in answer.

I shook my head and stood up. "Well, I've got things to do, I'd better go see if Uncle Jasper's ready to go."

I walked up just as Aunt Sarah was hugging everybody good-bye. Uncle Jasper put his hand on my shoulder and we ambled toward the car.

"What's wrong Joe Ben?"

"Oh, nothing."

"Come on now. If your lip was swelled out any more you'd be stepping on it."

"It's just Junebug. I asked him to go fishing and instead he's hanging around with that sappy Carolyn Jenkins and her cousin Danielle telling them how brave he is."

54

"Is that all? I remember somebody who didn't think Carolyn was so sappy a few months ago."

"That was different. I hung around with her when there wasn't anything else to do, Junebug's turning down a chance to go fishing. That's not normal."

Uncle Jasper chuckled.

"You know Joe Ben, in all the time you've been friends with him that may be the first normal thing I've ever seen Junebug Walker do."

# CHAPTER 7

The next week and a half was nearly intolerable. A heat wave seized St. John, turning a miserably hot summer into a stifling one. I wanted to spend my time at the creek or the pond, but all Junebug wanted to do was hang around Danielle. To make matters worse, Carolyn had started making eyes at me again and let me know she was amenable to the idea of a boyfriend, if I was so inclined.

I wasn't.

I sure hope I never act the way Junebug does around Danielle. Every now and then he gets this look on his face like he's a million miles away. That, in itself, isn't unusual since Miss Bunion says if his mind spent as much time in class as his body does he'd probably make straight A's. The difference was that now when he got that look it was accompanied by a goofy smile, and usually a sigh like you see on cartoons and in the movies when somebody falls in love. It'd look pitiful even if Junebug wasn't funny looking.

I was hanging around the sheriff's office one day trying to think of something to do when the telephone rang.

Cecil was asleep again and started struggling to sit up in the chair, but Uncle Jasper just looked disgusted and answered the telephone himself.

"Hello."

A pause while he listened to the other end.

"Yes, this is the Sheriff. I'll hold."

He put his hand over the receiver and whispered to me, "This is the coroner, Dr. Everett. He's calling with the lab reports on Mr. Duval. Do you want to listen in?"

I nodded my head and he held the handset away from his ear a little bit where I could hear.

"Sheriff, Donald Everett here. You sent a body down here a few weeks ago for an autopsy. Do you remember?"

"Yes sir. We don't have that many bodies turn up in these parts."

"I'd imagine not. Well, I'm calling because I finally got all the results back and am going to be preparing my final report but it may take awhile and I imagine you're going to want to get to work on this."

"Why's that?"

"From the condition of the body it was apparent it had been in the water a little while, although not long enough for decomposition to be very advanced. My educated guess would be two days at the most."

"That would fit in with the last date he was seen and when the body was found."

"Good, I'll make a note of that for my report." He paused and I could hear him flipping pages. "My physical examination of the body didn't reveal any evidence of foul play. There were some abrasions, but these were consistent with a body being dragged along a sandy creek bottom and occasionally hitting rocks or logs. Of course, there were no obvious signs to indicate anything out of the ordinary, like gunshot wounds, knife wounds, or anything like that."

"So your opinion is this was an accidental death?"

"I didn't say that. There was water in the lungs along with trace amounts of weeds and sand, again consistent with someone that has either drowned or been in the water for a while. The stomach contained the same water and materials as the lungs, but also had a small amount of partially digested food. I sent this along with tissue and blood samples off for testing and they came back a little unexpected."

"Why's that?"

57

"All of the samples showed a high concentration of a drug called Flurazapam, more commonly known as Dalmane. This is a fairly powerful medication commonly prescribed as a sleeping pill. I'd say somebody slipped your boy a mickey."

"Could it have been a suicide?"

"Possibly. Dalmane is a 'drug of choice', if you will, for suicides, usually in combination with another method of death like gassing by carbon monoxide or even drowning. The only real way to tell is to see if you can find out how he ingested the drug and then of course the circumstances surrounding the death".

"What do you mean?"

"He had to get it into his body somehow. I'd suggest you check and see if he ate or drank anything right before he died. If you find out he swallowed a handful of pills then that's a strong indication he killed himself. If, instead, you found out somebody had spiked a drink with that same handful it would indicate foul play."

"How long would it take for Dalmane to act on a person?"

"In the dose he must have ingested I'd say he felt the effects within five to ten minutes and was probably unconscious in no more than twenty. You see, Dalmane affects the central nervous system causing the victim's breathing to be impaired due to a decreased respiratory drive. Since they're not taking in enough oxygen they become groggy and pass out. In a sufficient dose it can even cause the breathing to stop completely."

"So he would have had to have been drugged shortly before he entered the water?"

"Yes, I'd say so. Unless of course somebody carried or dragged him from somewhere else."

"We found a half eaten tuna fish sandwich and a can of soda at the scene where we believe he was located right before whatever happened."

"Did you save these?"

"We have the sandwich in the freezer, but not the can."

"Why don't you put the sandwich in a cooler with some ice and have someone drive it down. I can run the tests here, now that we know what we're looking for."

"I'll send my deputy right down."

Uncle Jasper hung up.

"Cecil, you've got work to do."

*****************************

A storm blew in that night and Uncle Jasper had to go out in the driving rain to handle a wreck on the highway. He picked me up at 9:00 the next morning, dropping by the house in the patrol car.

"Where's Junebug?"

I shrugged.

"He'll sure hate to miss this. Dr. Everett just called. The tuna fish sandwich contained Dalmane. That must have been how he was drugged."

"So does that mean..."

"Well, it seem to me that if he was going to kill himself it'd be a lot easier just to swallow a handful of pills rather than grinding them up to put into a sandwich. It looks like Mr. Duval was murdered."

"Where are we going?"

"I thought we'd head over to Bessie's and take another look at the room, then see if Mrs. Duval's still there."

Mrs. Hardeman let us into the room and Uncle Jasper went straight to a briefcase on the floor, opening it and digging through the papers inside. He pulled one bundle out and inspected it closer.

After a minute he stood and walked out the door, holding the papers he'd been looking at.

"Is Mrs. Duval still here?"

"She's in her room. Third one on the right."

Uncle Jasper knocked.

"Yes? Who is it?" A voice said from behind the door.

"It's the Sheriff. I need to talk to you Mrs. Duval."

"Can you come back a little later?"

"No ma'am. I need to talk to you right now."

"I'll be right out. I just need to get dressed."

"We'll wait for you downstairs."

We sat down on the couch in the parlor to wait. Just as we were getting comfortable the front door opened and Junebug came strutting in.

"Hey, did y'all forget me?"

"No, I just figured you were too busy with Danielle to be interested in helping us."

"Nah, she had to go to Sumter today to visit another aunt. I've got plenty of time. Why was that lady crawling out of the window upstairs?"

"Do what?" Uncle Jasper jumped up and ran out the door with us following.

Mrs. Duval was standing on the roof that extended from below the second floor windows and which provided a covering for the porch. She was leaning over, apparently looking for a way down.

"That's a long jump Mrs. Duval. I wouldn't try it with those high heels."

While we were standing there looking up at Mrs. Duval looking down at us, a car stopped on the street.

"Say, what's going on here?" Scoop Brown yelled after he rolled down his window.

"Nothing Scoop. Just talking to Mrs. Duval," Uncle Jasper responded.

"Y'all mind if I hang around? Might be something I could use for the paper."

My uncle seldom cursed but I heard him mumble under his breath, "Shit."

Scoop walked up and stood beside us.

Mrs. Duval shrugged and climbed back through the open window into her room.

************************

The parlor was getting crowded. Uncle Jasper and Mrs. Duval sat facing each other in the two chairs, while me, Scoop and Junebug huddled on the couch.

"Did you kill your husband?" Uncle Jasper asked.

"What's he talking about? Why does he think she killed him? What's going on? Answer me, Joe Ben!" Junebug whispered frantically.

"Hush, Junebug! Just listen and I'll explain later."

I thought I saw a look of amusement cross Mrs. Duval's face momentarily before it settled into a shocked expression.

"Sheriff, I loved my husband."

"But you were separated."

"Not living together does not equal not loving each other. It's like I told you, we were much better friends than we were spouses."

"Mrs. Duval, I talked to the coroner yesterday and he said your husband had a high concentration of Dalmane in his body at the time of his death."

"Dalmane?"

"Yes, Mrs. Duval. Are you familiar with it?"

She stared at Uncle Jasper for an instant. "I suppose you'll find out anyway. Yes, I'm familiar with Dalmane."

"How?"

"I've had a prescription for a few years. It helps me to sleep."

"Do you have any of them with you?"

She opened her purse and took out a pill bottle handing it to him.

"This prescription was refilled last month?"

"That's right."

61

"It looks like it was a three months supply."

"It was supposed to be."

"Looks like it's about half empty."

"I've had to double up lately. I've built up a bit of a tolerance."

"Tell me again what you did on the last day you saw Mr. Duval alive."

"I'd driven up to see if he wanted to have lunch. He told me he was going out to the woods to write again since he only had a few chapters left on his new book and it was due in a few days."

"Didn't you mention something about buying his lunch for him?"

"Why's he asking all these questions, Joe Ben?" Junebug whispered again.

"Shut up and listen," I whispered back.

She snapped her fingers. "That's right, I forgot. Ted asked me to run to the drugstore and get him a tuna fish sandwich, so I did. We talked for a minute and then I left. I got the impression he was leaving right after me."

Uncle Jasper just stared at her, obviously thinking things through.

"Why all the questions, Sheriff? If you're wondering about the Dalmane, Ted occasionally took one when he needed to get a good night's sleep."

"He only took one when he was having trouble?"

"Yes, he was very precise on that. He said if he took more than one in a night or more than one or two nights in a row he felt groggy for a day or two and couldn't write."

Scoop was scribbling on that little notepad of his with the pencil stub. He was writing so fast I'm surprised smoke wasn't coming off the end of the pencil.

"Mrs. Duval, your husband's body contained a large amount of Dalmane, far more than would be present if he'd only taken one the night before."

"What are you trying to say?"

"It's very simple. It looks like your husband was murdered. Somebody loaded his sandwich with those sleeping pills."

"Surely you don't think I did it?"

"Ma'am, you were the one who got it for him, you had a prescription for the drug, naturally it looks mighty suspicious."

Junebug was sitting there with his mouth open.

"What possible reason could I have for wanting to murder my husband?"

"I've seen people do things for a lot of different reasons, but it seems like jealousy, anger, and money are the three most common. Since you weren't living together, jealousy probably isn't it. Bessie Hardeman didn't hear y'all arguing and she hears everything, Right Bessie?" Uncle Jasper looked up and at the doorway. We could hear Mrs. Hardeman snort and quickly stomp away from where she had apparently been listening, unknown to anyone except him.

"Like I was saying, she'd have heard if y'all were arguing so I'm going to rule out anger for right now. That only leaves money."

"I assume you're headed somewhere with this?"

"Yes ma'am. Do you have any idea how much Mr. Duval was worth?"

"Roughly. I believe he told me he had a little more than a hundred thousand dollars stashed away here and there."

"Have you ever seen this before?" He handed her the sheaf of papers he'd taken from the briefcase.

She glanced at the documents momentarily, then handed them back. "I've seen them."

"It looks to me like you stood to inherit his entire estate if he died."

63

She shook her head. "I didn't kill him."

"Then why were you trying to run?"

"It didn't sound like you. I was scared."

"What do you have to be scared of?"

She hesitated for a moment, then reached into her purse and pulled out a letter.

"A few weeks before he died, Ted sent this to me."

Uncle Jasper took it from her and read it, stopping suddenly and looking up.

"Is he serious?"

"That's what I asked him. He said he was."

He folded the letter and put it back into the envelope, then started to place it in his pocket.

"Sheriff, would you mind if I looked at that?" Scoop asked, holding his hand out.

Uncle Jasper looked at the outstretched hand, then at Mrs. Duval, who nodded her head. He placed the letter in Scoop's hand.

As he opened it Junebug jumped down and walked to stand next to the reporter where he could read the letter at the same time. I leaned over so I could see as well.

Dear Julia:

I'm writing this letter in case something happens to me. I'm afraid I've stumbled into something over my head with this last book. Apparently there are some people who don't want the truth known about what happened in St. John that fateful day in 1952.

I've seen someone following me for the last few days and feel like something's about to happen. If I disappear or pass away please find my manuscript and get it to my publisher, but be very careful. I don't want anything to happen to you.

Love, your favorite husband,
Ted

"Jeez," Scoop remarked.

"So you see why I was scared?" Mrs. Duval asked.

"I see why you want us to think you were scared. This manuscript he was talking about, did you see it?"

"No. The room's been locked and Mrs. Hardeman wouldn't let me inside."

"What would it look like?"

"I know he was a few days away from finishing it up on the last day I saw him, so it would most probably be a stack of yellow notepads, probably a dozen or more. He was very superstitious about his writing and refused to change anything."

"What do you mean?"

"Well, I told you about the special pen he used and the yellow pads. He refused to start typing his manuscript until he was completely finished and then he'd start typing the last chapter first, and work his way backwards until he finished. He also wore the same old fashioned reading glasses when he wrote even though he had a pair of contact lenses he wore for everything else. I doubt very seriously if he changed anything so I'd start looking for those tablets."

"There's a problem."

"What's that?"

"Somebody apparently ransacked his room. The tablets are missing."

She put her hand to her mouth. "Oh my god, he was telling the truth."

"We don't know that for sure yet. All I do know is my simple little drowning case gets more and more complicated all the time."

"Don't worry Sheriff. You can count on me and Joe Ben helping you." Junebug volunteered.

"See what I mean?" Uncle Jasper said to no one in particular.

65

# CHAPTER 8

St. John was famous!

Poor Scoop Brown had written his story and put it out over the news wire services, forgetting that his paper didn't publish until the weekend. This meant the story, which made almost every major newspaper in the country, was published last of all by the St. John Jimplecute. By the time the local paper came out the town was crawling with reporters and curiosity hounds.

Every spare room in town, with the exception of the one in our house, was rented out and reporters were having to drive to the county seat of Sumter, almost twenty miles away to find hotel rooms.

Bessie Hardeman called Uncle Jasper the first day.

"Jasper, I'm just going to have to rent that room out. I've got people offering me five and six times the usual rent so they can stay in the room Mr. Duval had."

"We can't rent it out yet. This is a murder and there's an investigation going on."

"Do you know how much money you're costing me? That's not fair."

"How much does that room usually rent for?"

"Thirty five dollars a week, meals included."

"I tell you what I'll do, either the town or the county will agree to pay you fifty dollars a week for as long as we have to keep the room sealed."

"Fifty dollars a week! I can get lots more than that."

"Yes, but it's more than you usually charge and you don't have to feed it. Don't get greedy Bessie or I'll seal off the whole house as an evidence scene."

I knew he wouldn't do that but apparently Mrs.

Hardeman didn't because she hung up and I saw Uncle Jasper make a note to start sending her the money.

I decided to head over to Junebug's house, splashing through the puddles that remained from the rain last night, and see what he thought about all of the excitement. As I got closer I could see cars parked along the street and a crowd of people gathered in front of his house.

There was a big cardboard box set up on Junebug's lawn, with a sign on the front that said "Eyewitness Reports $1.00 per ten minutes". Junebug was sitting behind the box in a folding chair. He waved at me when I walked up.

"Hey Joe Ben, have a seat." He unfolded another chair next to him and then stood on his to address the crowd.

"Folks you're in luck, Joe Ben here was with me during the entire investigation. I'm going to have to ask you for another dollar each since you're going to be getting twice the information."

"But we've already paid you once," somebody yelled out from the crowd.

"Sorry folks, twice the information, twice the charge. Anybody that wants a refund can have one by leaving their address and telephone number and I'll be glad to mail it to them, however, anybody that doesn't want to invest two dollars in hearing from the only two people in the world that have been involved with this case from the beginning will be asked to leave. And I'll remind you that Joe Ben's uncle is the sheriff and won't take kindly to strangers trying to take advantage of our youth and inexperience."

He turned and grinned at me than leaned down and whispered, "I've already made twenty bucks this morning. I'll give you your half later." He climbed down off of the chair and began passing through the crowd collecting the money. A minor altercation started when Junebug told some fellow in a suit that he didn't

remember him having already paid and so he owed
$2.00. The man objected at first then sheepishly handed
over the $2.00 when others in the crowd started
hollering for him to stop being a cheapskate and that he
was holding everything up. A few more dollars were
paid when Junebug would stop and stare suspiciously at
a member of the crowd for a few seconds, moving on
only after they forked over an extra dollar.

Eventually Junebug returned to his place, and
stood there hopping from foot to foot.

"What are you waiting on?" I asked him in a
whisper.

"Sure is hot today, isn't it?" He asked with a grin
and looked down the street.

Carolyn and Danielle were coming down the
sidewalk pulling a red wagon filled with ice in which
someone had put a couple of pitchers of lemonade and
some bottles of Coca-Cola.

People lined up at the wagon, some opting for
lemonade and others for the soft drinks, and within
minutes the wagon was empty and the girls had
disappeared back the way they'd came, pockets bulging
with money.

"They'll be back in a little while. I told them
we'd split the profits they made, half for us and half for
them."

"What about the money for talking to these
guys?"

"That's ours. Shoot, they weren't with us, were
they?"

He handed me a stopwatch, climbed onto the
chair again and waved his arms.

"All right folks, I'll talk for the first five minutes
and then me and Joe Ben will answer questions for the
next five. Ready?"

The crowd almost as one yelled, "Yes!"

"It started on a day earlier this summer, but not
quite as hot as this one. Joe Ben and I decided to go

68

catfishing out at Sandy Creek but the fish weren't biting so we...."

His story again made him sound braver than I remembered, but after all it was his story and we were making a gob of money from it.

At exactly five minutes I jabbed him in the leg and climbed up onto my chair so they could talk to both of us.

\*\*\*\*\*\*\*\*\*\*\*\*\*\*\*\*\*\*\*\*

"How much did we make this morning?"

"All told, including drinks and everything we made a little over a hundred dollars to split between us."

"Gosh Junebug, if this keeps up we'll be rich by the end of summer. Finding that body was the best thing that ever happened to us."

We were sitting on the corner out in front of the sheriff's office waiting for Uncle Jasper to get back. Our crowd had dwindled by noon, although Junebug had started talking slower and managed to make it take two of the ten minute segments to get the whole story.

We'd decided to come down to visit Uncle Jasper and hopefully get some new information to incorporate into our performance.

"You know, those reporters told me your uncle wouldn't talk to them at all. I bet if we could persuade him they'd pay ten dollars to hear it."

"I don't know if he'd go for that, Junebug. You know how touchy he is about his job."

"Aw, we'd split the money with him. We could schedule his talk at the hottest part of the afternoon and make up the difference on the drinks. Do you think he'd be interested?"

A shadow fell across us just then and Uncle Jasper's voice said from behind us, "Nope, he sure wouldn't. Why don't you boys come inside and tell me exactly what you've been up to this morning?"

\*\*\*\*\*\*\*\*\*\*\*\*\*\*\*\*\*\*\*\*\*\*

"Where do you get these ideas from Junebug?"
Uncle Jasper asked after we'd explained how
industrious we'd been.

"I don't know, they just come to me."

"Do you ever stop to think before you act on
them?"

"Why would I want to do that? If I thought too
long I might come up with a reason not to."

My uncle just shook his head.

"Boys, I admire your ambition but you're going
to have to make a choice, either you can help me or you
can run your business, but you can't do both. A lot of
what I do and know has to be kept secret until the crime
is solved or else it might ruin the investigation. Do you
understand?"

We both nodded our heads.

"Well, which is it?"

"We want to help you," Junebug said and I
agreed.

"All right then, no more press conferences or
anything else unless you ask me first."

Junebug raised his hand.

"You don't have to raise your hand, what do you
want?"

He reached into his back pocket and pulled out a
smudged piece of paper with some lines drawn on it
and handed it to Uncle Jasper.

"What's this?"

"It's a map I drew of how to get out to Sandy
Creek and where everything happened out there. We
had Mr. Stanton over to the print shop make us a
hundred copies and were going to sell them. Is that all
right?"

Uncle Jasper rubbed his temples with both
hands as if he were getting a headache.

"Is there anything else?"

"No, that's it."

"Not planning on writing a book or giving guided tours or anything?"

Junebug looked thoughtful. "No, I hadn't thought of that."

"Well, don't. You can finish selling these but then no more of anything else."

He leaned back in his chair. "There isn't much we can do in the way of investigating until these yay-hoos leave town. Why don't you two boys run over to Bessie's and see if Mr. Duval got his mail there."

"Yes Chief."

Junebug saluted and headed for the door.

Uncle Jasper opened his mouth to say something, but then stopped and shook his head. He just watched us as we left the office.

\*\*\*\*\*\*\*\*\*\*\*\*\*\*\*\*\*\*\*\*\*\*\*\*\*\*\*\*\*

"I think his wife did it," Junebug said as we walked across town.

"What makes you think that?"

"She had the sleeping pills, she got his sandwich for him and she inherits a bunch of money when he dies. That's a lot of evidence."

"What about that letter? Mr. Duval thought he had somebody else after him."

"We don't know if that was really a letter from him, she could have made that up."

"I don't think she did it. She doesn't look like a murderer."

"Dang it Joe Ben, don't you watch TV? The one that does it never looks like they're the ones that did it. When are you ever gonna learn?"

We continued our walk in silence, eventually turning into the walkway at Mrs. Hardeman's. Junebug knocked on the door and stepped back to wait for her to answer.

"I still don't think she did it," I said just as I heard Mrs. Hardeman start to turn the knob. Her opening the door cut off Junebug's chance to argue.

"Mrs. Hardeman, we're here on official business. The sheriff sent us to find out if Mr. Duval got any mail while he was staying here."

"Why didn't he come himself rather than sending you two?"

"I guess he was just too busy with important sheriff stuff."

"Is he any closer to solving the case?"

I spoke up. "I'm sorry Mrs. Hardeman, we're not allowed to discuss that with anyone."

"That's confidential ma'am," Junebug said at almost the same time. "Now could you answer the sheriff's question?"

"You can tell Jasper that Mr. Duval did get mail while he was here."

We started to leave but Junebug stopped all of a sudden and turned back to her.

"Has any mail came in since he disappeared?"

"I'm not sure, I'd have to check." She didn't move.

Junebug plopped himself back down in a chair.

"We'll wait here while you do."

"It may take me a while, I'm not sure where I would have put it."

He reached over and picked up one of the numerous knick-knacks scattered around the room.

"That's all right, we'll just look around."

"Junebug Walker, don't you touch anything. I'll be right back." She hurried out of the room and reappeared a moment later with a few envelopes. "Here, take these to Jasper...and mind you don't break anything on the way out."

On the way out of the house one of the reporters who I recognized as having been in the crowd and paid $2.00 to hear us was coming up the sidewalk.

72

"Hi boys, what are you doing?"

Junebug held his hand up as if he was a traffic cop stopping cars and said as he continued walking, "Sorry mister, we don't have time to talk now, we're on official police business."

"Is that right? What have y'all got there?" He reached into his pocket and pulled out his billfold.

You couldn't have stopped Junebug any quicker if you'd lassoed him.

"These are letters that came to Mr. Duval after he died, so his landlady kept them."

"Where are you taking them?"

"Junebug, let's go." I pulled on his arm.

"We're taking them to the sheriff."

"What kind of letters are they?"

"Don't know, they haven't been opened yet."

"Come on, Uncle Jasper's waiting on us." I pulled harder but only managed to knock Junebug off balance. He quickly stood up straight again.

"You know, there's probably not anything there except bills or junk mail, but I'd be willing to pay $20.00 to have a look at them."

"Twenty dollars?" It was obvious this was a sum Junebug took seriously.

I pulled on his arm again and he looked at me then regretfully said, "I'm sorry mister, but I can't, they're the property of the sheriff's office now and it wouldn't be right."

"I'll make it fifty dollars."

"Fifty dollars? Joe Ben, we need to talk about this." He pulled me to the side.

"No we don't. Junebug do you want to spend the rest of the summer sitting on your porch and watching Uncle Jasper and me drive back and forth working on this case?" I whispered.

"Of course not," he whispered back.

"Well then, let's go. If Uncle Jasper finds out we've even talked to this man he may cut us out."

73

"But fifty dollars? Joe Ben, that's twenty five dollars apiece."

"I know how much it is. Who made an A in arithmetic and who made a C? Now hand me that mail," I yanked it out of his hands, "and let's go...now."

I started running back to the sheriff's office. Within a few yards Junebug had caught up and was running next to me.

"Thanks. I just don't have any will power when it comes to refusing money."

"Junebug, you don't have any will power when it comes to refusing anything you want."

Uncle Jasper was still sitting behind his desk when we ran in.

"Well, what'd the old harpy say?"

"She said he got mail while he was there. Junebug also got her to give us this." I handed him the envelopes. "This is mail that's come in since he left."

"Good work boys. Junebug, that was a good idea, I should have thought of that."

The first three letters were junk mail, but Uncle Jasper made a point of carefully putting them back into their original envelopes and then placing these into a large brown one.

It was quickly apparent the next envelope was different.

"I'll be damned," he mumbled after scanning the letter.

He leaned back in his chair and rubbed his eyes, just like he did when Junebug was getting on his nerves.

"What's wrong?" I asked.

"We just got another suspect in the murder."

# CHAPTER 9

"Who?" Junebug and I both yelled at the same instant.

As he waved the letter Junebug made a grab for it, missing by an inch as Uncle Jasper held it out of his reach.

"Sit down and wait and I'll read it to you. I don't want you to get your grubby little hands all over it in case we need to try and take fingerprints or something." He carefully held the sheet of paper by one corner and began to read:

"Dear Mr. Duval,

"Mystery Train" made a sack full of advance money for you, money which rightfully belonged to me since I wrote the book. I don't know how you thought you would manage to keep anyone from discovering you had plagiarized but it appears your ego hasn't gotten any smaller since you were teaching the writing class.

If you would have simply told me you were interested in my ghost writing for you, or in purchasing the rights to the book I would have made a deal that was very favorable to you since I needed the money and would have liked the experience and prestige of working with you. Instead, you choose to steal my final assignment from the class, make a very few minor changes, and release it under a different name.

This industry is filled with crooks like you and I have had enough. Since you won't respond to my letters I have no choice but to come in person. Hopefully, this matter can be resolved peacefully but if not, just remember I told you I wouldn't give up until I saw that justice was done.
Sincerely,
Joshua Lamonto

"Gosh Uncle Jasper, do you think whoever wrote that killed Mr. Duval?"

"Joe Ben, I don't know who killed him. All I know is my suspect list is narrowed down to his wife, this feller," he waggled the letter, "and anybody that might have committed the robbery. The way I see it that would include everybody that was born after about 1936."

"Where do you want us to start, Chief?" Junebug asked.

"Nowhere. I said y'all could watch and listen and help out by running errands and such but do not," he leaned down and shifted his gaze back and forth between Junebug's eyes, looking into each one for at least a moment as he said this, "*do not* do anything else unless I tell you to."

"Right, Chief," Junebug replied as chipper as ever.

"And don't call me Chief. Now y'all go find something to do and let me get some peace and quiet for the rest of the day so I can figure things out."

Junebug saluted and we left to try our luck at perch jerking in Weaver's Pond.

\*\*\*\*\*\*\*\*\*\*\*\*\*\*\*\*\*\*\*\*\*\*\*\*\*\*\*\*\*\*

Things were quiet in St. John for the next couple of days as Uncle Jasper waited for the reporters to clear out before continuing his investigation.

Mrs. Duval agreed to stay in town until he said otherwise. She was bothered by the newspaper people for a while, and took to staying in her room most of the time.

The few exceptions to her seclusion were errands and appearances at the society gatherings in town. For some reason she became a favorite speaker and guest at the Tea Society, the Ladies Auxiliary, and the Garden Society as well as all the others.

One Saturday morning Uncle Jasper came stomping into the kitchen where I was eating breakfast with Aunt Sarah. He had a copy of the latest edition of the St. John Jimplecute wadded in his hand.

"Sarah, what in the world are you doing?"

"What are you talking about?"

"This," he waved the paper in the air. "It says here 'The St. John Garden Society will be meeting Tuesday at the home of Jasper and Sarah Johnson. The topic will be orchids and the featured speaker is renowned poet Julia Duval'."

"So?"

"So? So? That woman is a suspect in a murder I'm investigating."

"Jasper, you have your business and I have mine. It so happens Mrs. Duval is a very intelligent woman who has had her poetry published in several books and magazines. Since she appears to be staying here I thought asking her to attend was the neighborly thing to do."

"For God's sake Sarah, she's not the new school teacher, she's suspected of murdering her husband. You don't have to be neighborly."

"I'm not going to be rude, Jasper. If she's living in St. John she has every right to take part in our organizations."

"She's not living here, she's been ordered to stay here. Ordered, incidentally, by me, your husband and the sheriff in this county."

Uncle Jasper shook his head and sat in one of the kitchen chairs prompting Aunt Sarah to grab her fancy china cup from where it sat in front of him, empty, and replacing it with a chipped porcelain mug that she considered safe for him to use.

"Woman, between you and Junebug Walker I'll be lucky if I don't have a stroke before the summer is over. How do you think it looks for the wife of the sheriff to be hosting a party with the guest of honor being someone I may have to put in prison? What are people going to say?"

"They're going to say 'Look there, isn't Sarah Johnson gracious? Just because her husband Jasper is being unsociable is no reason for her to be'. Besides," Aunt Sarah got a pleased expression on her face, "she's already turned down Louetta's invitation to read some of her poetry at the tea next week."

Louetta Mae Hopkins was Aunt Sarah's chief rival in town. When they were together in public you would think they were best friends and so sweet to each other sugar wouldn't melt in their mouths, but when you separated them they were bitter enemies.

The feud had started seven years before when the two women were vying for top honors in the sweet potato pie contest at the Pine Cone festival over in Sumter.

Aunt Sarah's pies had beaten Louetta's out by the narrowest of margins for four years running. She was determined to make it five in a row and had sent Uncle Jasper all the way to Dallas to buy special potatoes she had been assured were the closest thing available to nectar of the gods.

There were two schools of thought and two different categories depending on how a sweet potato pie was baked. Aunt Sarah was from the denomination who believed in using spices and extra ingredients in her pies. Louetta Mae Hopkins championed the second faction, who espoused a pure pie, relying solely on the flavor of the potato and the cook's ability to extract the most sweetness from the bright orange tuber. At the festival, the winner of each of the categories then competed for best overall.

The day of the big pie judging came and the field was quickly narrowed to Aunt Sarah and her nemesis. To the winner would go the blue ribbon and an assortment of Watkins spices, while the loser would slink home in defeat, bearing only a red ribbon with the words "Honorable Mention" emblazoned on it, informing the entire world of her shame.

I noticed Uncle Jasper and Hollis Hopkins, Louetta's husband, standing over to the side grinning and laughing as if some great joke were taking place. Mr. Hopkins pulled a small brown bottle out of his pocket and showed the label to Uncle Jasper, whose grin got bigger.

This year the judging was being conducted by Brother Larry Haymond, preacher at the First Baptist Church, Father Flaherty of the Catholic Church in Sumter, and State Senator Owen Hampton, who had represented Baldwin County in the State legislature for a zillion years.

The three judges strode up the steps to the judging area, where a member of the Ladies Auxiliary solemnly handed each two small paper plates. In the center of each of the plates was a portion of sweet potato pie too small to be considered more than a taste.

As if on cue, all three lifted a bite of the first pie to their lips. It was obvious from the expressions that passed between them the entry was more than acceptable and they whispered back and forth while making notes on their scorecards. After a moment, they took a swig of water to rinse their mouths then tasted the second piece.

Brother Haymond stood for a moment as if puzzled, then slowly chewed his mouthful, a smile spreading across his face. Father Flaherty remained

79

impassive as he completed his task, while Senator Hampton leaned over and helped himself to another, bigger piece of the second entry, devouring it as quickly as he had the minuscule amount they'd first given him.

A brief discussion and the announcement was made.

"By unanimous decision, this year's first place ribbon and prize goes to...Louetta Mae Hopkins."

I thought Aunt Sarah was about to pass out and from the look on her face you'd have thought Doc West had just told her Prissy was about to be the proud mother of a litter of Jake's pups.

Mrs. Hopkins climbed to the grandstand and smiled sweetly down at Aunt Sarah, who turned and left, dabbing at her eyes with her handkerchief.

I watched her go and happened to catch a glimpse of Uncle Jasper who was choking and gagging and eventually spit out a fairly large hunk of the cigar he'd been chewing and had apparently nearly swallowed when the announcement was made.

After the crowd cleared out I ambled over to near where he and Hollis were standing hunkered over and whispering.

"...I swear Jasper, I did."

"You know she's gonna kill me if she ever finds out."

"I sure won't tell her. Do you know what Louetta would do to me?"

"What in the world happened?"

"I put nearly the whole bottle in there."

"I'd have never thought a little bit of whiskey would make that much difference."

"Brother Haymond sure enjoyed it."

"Yeah and I thought the Senator would lick the plate."

"Do you know what my life is gonna be like now?"

Mr. Hopkins took off his hat and wiped his head with the handkerchief he'd pulled from the pocket of his bib overalls.

"*Your* life? Good God, now Louetta won't ever stop making those damned things. I hate sweet potato pies but I have to try out every new recipe she comes up with. She'd said if she lost this year she wouldn't enter again."

Uncle Jasper took a step back at that point and bumped into me.

We looked at each other a second, then he said, "I won't tell her about the snake if you won't tell her about this."

I stuck my hand out.

"Deal."

To this day Aunt Sarah still doesn't know how Louetta beat her. But the animosity between the two continues and each grabs every chance they can to one-up the other.

"Well it just isn't right, that's all. You don't see me palling up to that thief Horace Briggs just because he knows where the best fishing spots in Baldwin County are, do you?"

"Jasper, you not liking Horace hasn't got anything to do with him stealing that goat. You've had a grudge against him since I went with him instead of you to the barn dance back in high school."

"Dadburn it Sarah, that isn't the point. I can't have my wife consorting with a suspected felon. It's not proper."

"Haven't you always told me a person is innocent until proven guilty?"

"Well, yes."

"Does that just apply to people you're not investigating?"

"Of course not."

"Fine then. I refuse to take part in your attempts to deprive St. John of what little culture we can embrace. Mrs. Duval will speak as planned."

Uncle Jasper turned red and left the kitchen. I could hear his recliner squeak as he dropped into it. Wisely, I sat in silence until I could finish eating and slip out the back door.

\*\*\*\*\*\*\*\*\*\*\*\*\*\*\*\*\*\*\*\*\*\*\*\*\*\*\*\*\*\*

Mrs. Walker told me Junebug was off somewhere with Danielle, courting I assume, so I decided to head to the library and curl up with a good book in the air conditioning.

I picked up the latest issue of Field and Stream from the rack and sat down at one of the tables, opposite a reporter who was paging through some clippings in a manila folder.

After a while I looked up and he was gone along with his camera and notebooks, leaving the folder closed on the table. Out of curiosity I pulled it toward me and opened it.

Staring back from the first clipping was a face I had seen before, although it had been waterlogged and lying on the bank of Sandy Creek at the time.

The folder contained a handful of clippings from various magazines and newspapers and had Ted Duval's name on the tab.

Reluctantly, since she was never able to keep from pinching my cheeks when she saw me, I picked it up and went looking for the librarian.

"Mrs. Augustine, what's this?"

"Why Joe Ben Johnson, how are you doing?"

"Just fine Mrs. Augustine. I found this...."

"How are your Uncle Jasper and Aunt Sarah?"

"They're just fine. This folder..."

"Aren't you getting to be a handsome young man?" Here came the pinch. "I swear every time I see you it's like you've grown a foot taller."

"Yes'm. I was asking about..."

"And how is Junebug? Such a peculiar little boy, but my how he can read. You be sure and tell him we miss him this summer and that he'd better start coming by or he won't win the contest this year."

Mrs. Augustine had obviously missed the day in librarian's school where they taught you a library was supposed to be a quiet place without a lot of talking.

"I'll be sure and tell him."

She opened her mouth to say something else and on impulse, I dropped the file on the floor, scattering clippings right and left.

"I'm sorry."

"That's all right. Let me help you pick them up."

As she shut up to kneel down I saw my chance.

"Mrs. Augustine, exactly what is this?"

"This is what we call a vertical file. Most libraries either belong to a clipping service or go through the papers and magazines themselves looking for items of local interest. Since I happened to know Theodore Duval when he lived here I've been keeping up with this since the review of his first book."

We replaced all of the papers into the file and she was just getting ready to launch into another series of questions and stories when someone walked up to the counter with an armload of books and she bustled away.

As Mrs. Augustine had said the articles tracked Mr. Duval's career from his first novel until recently. There was a blurb about his marriage to Julia Duval and another about the separation. An article from the society and gossip section of the Dallas Post told of him being hospitalized earlier this year after blacking out at a restaurant and being carried away in an ambulance. That was the last thing prior to the avalanche of stories concerning his death.

# CHAPTER 10

I was just leaving the library when I saw
Junebug running down the opposite side of the street,
headed in the direction of my house.

"Hey," I yelled.

Without slowing his pace he turned to look at
me and waved. Unfortunately, he started to change
direction a fraction of a second too late and plowed into
the door of a truck just as Mrs. Hanscomb opened it and
stepped out.

At the speed Junebug was traveling he'd have
had a good chance of just blasting on through with little
harm if Mrs. Hanscomb hadn't been standing against
the door.

She was a large woman, partial to pork and
collard greens and known to have a fondness for Schlitz
beer. Since Baldwin County was "dry", one of Mr.
Hanscomb's husbandly duties was to drive to Louisiana
and bring back a supply of hooch for his lady fair.
Personally, if I had to be married to Mrs. Hanscomb I
think it'd be more likely I'd be the one to have a taste
for booze.

The only type of clothes I ever saw her wear
was one of those tent dresses, yellow with big blue
flowers all over it. During the summer she also wore a
straw hat with plastic flowers and carried a matching
purse.

Although I'm sure she didn't open the door into
him on purpose, Mrs. Hanscomb and Junebug had been
mortal enemies since he had started spreading the
rumor that her hat had two ear holes cut into it, which
he insisted was absolute proof the hat had been worn by
their mule before she'd confiscated it.

Junebug hit the open door with a resounding "WHOMP" and rebounded several feet before falling to the pavement on his back.

"Oh my god, I've killed him," Mrs. Hanscomb screamed before he'd hit the ground.

I ran across the street, careful to dodge out of old Miss Blair's way as she weaved back and forth on her daily drive to the Piggly Wiggly. I could tell it was Miss Blair because all you could see of the driver were two old hands gripping the steering wheel and a bun made of blue hair barely visible over the top of the dashboard.

By the time I made it to the other sidewalk Mrs. Hanscomb had sat down on the sidewalk and had Junebug cradled against her massive breasts.

"Oh help me Jesus, help me Jesus. I didn't mean to kill him, I swear I didn't."

I had some experience with dead bodies and was reasonably sure that if Junebug really had been dead he wouldn't have been frantically kicking his legs and waving his arms back and forth.

"Mrs. Hanscomb, I think he's all right."

She continued rocking back and forth with his head crammed securely between her left breast and armpit.

"I'm sorry, I'm sorry, I'm sorry. Oh Jesus, please let poor pitiful little Junebug be all right and I swear I'll never think mean thoughts about him again."

The kicking and struggling stopped suddenly, followed immediately by a scream from Mrs. Hanscomb and a shout from Junebug as the massive woman flung him to the side.

"He's done bit a hole in me. Look here Chester," Mrs. Hanscomb motioned toward a place on the side of her chest just under her armpit. "Is it bleeding?"

Her husband, a much braver person than me and obviously with a much stronger stomach, leaned down and lifted her arm to look at a spot on the yellow dress prominently marked by a large sweat stain then shook his head to indicate there wasn't any blood.

Junebug lay on the ground a few feet away gagging and gasping for air.

"Darn woman almost suffocated me," he said in between breaths.

"Are you all right?" I asked.

"Heck no." He wiped his hand across his mouth, then started spitting. "I don't think I'll ever get the taste of sweat out of my mouth." He grimaced.

"What were you thinking?"

He put his hands to the ground and slowly got to his feet. I could see a few fresh scrapes where he'd hit the sidewalk after his collision. He ignored them and stood there glaring at Mrs. Hanscomb, who had several men trying to help her to her feet.

"Doesn't that woman believe in taking a bath more than once a year?"

"Where were you headed in such a hurry anyway?"

He slapped his hand against his forehead.

"That's right, I almost forgot. I've found another suspect."

\*\*\*\*\*\*\*\*\*\*\*\*\*\*\*\*\*\*\*\*\*\*\*\*

"What are you talking about?"

"I stopped at the cafe and was sitting at the counter drinking my Coke when I glanced over at the table next to me. There was this big guy sitting there and wearing a tan jacket."

"So?"

"Don't interrupt. When he reached over for the salt I saw a newspaper he had in the pocket of his jacket. It had a picture of Ted Duval with a circle drawn around it in red." He looked pleased with himself.

"So what? Most of the reporters probably had copies of the articles with them. It doesn't mean he had anything to do with Mr. Duval getting killed."

"I know that, but this fellow looked suspicious. I waited until he finished his hamburger and followed him to his car. In the back seat there was a box full of papers and sitting right on top were two of Mr. Duval's books and do you know what else?"

"What?"

"He had a violin case."

"What in the heck does a violin case have to do with somebody being poisoned?"

"Don't you remember anything? In that gangster movie just a couple of weeks ago on television, what did they carry in their violin cases right before they robbed the bank?"

"Machine guns."

He just stared at me as I stared at him.

"Joe Ben, think! Didn't your Uncle Jasper say his suspects included the people that robbed the bank?"

"How many people have you seen in real life who carry guns in a violin case?"

"Well, none."

"You see?"

"How many bank robbers have you seen in real life?"

"None."

"See?"

"Junebug, I think you're letting your imagination run away with you again."

"Look, your uncle said you have to investigate all possibilities and you shouldn't have any notions about who is innocent or guilty when you're investigating, right?"

"I guess so."

"Then let's tail this guy for a while and see what happens. If I'm wrong, I'm wrong and we haven't lost anything."

I shrugged my shoulders. "Okay, it beats sitting around doing nothing. Where is he?"

"I saw him park in front and go into Mrs. Hardeman's boarding house right before I came looking for you. Let's see if he's still there."

We headed in that direction and as we turned the corner across the street, Junebug suddenly dove behind a bush dragging me with him.

"What'd you do that for?"

"Shhhh." He held a finger to his lips, then pointed across the street.

Through a small hole in the bush I could see a man walking down the sidewalk leading from the door of the boarding house. He was a huge man, way taller than my Uncle Jasper and big enough to have played on the offensive line of the Dallas Cowboys. His hair was jet black and he had one eyebrow that went all the way across his forehead.

The man crossed the street and opened the door to a brand new Chevrolet Impala parked a few feet from us. The car sunk under his weight as he climbed in and slammed the door. He was so close I could see a ring on his right pinkie and the thickest hair I'd ever seen on the back of somebody's fingers.

He started the car and pulled through the intersection, with me and Junebug crawling around the bush to keep it between us and him. He drove only a few feet further and stopped again, turning the engine off.

"What's he doing?"

"I don't know."

We watched him for a few minutes but couldn't see very much because of the sun glaring off the back window.

"Come on," Junebug said and started crawling on his hands and knees across the grass toward an alley that ran behind the house the man was parked in front of.

Personally, I thought it would be less likely to arouse suspicion if we'd just walked over, but I knew in

Junebug's mind we were Frank and Joe Hardy and they would never have done things the easy way. Plus, it would have offended his sense of melodrama to've simply ambled to another vantage point when crawling was an option.

Eventually, we made our way around the house although I stood and walked once we were safely behind it. Junebug stayed on his hands and knees until we made it to a set of hedges just in front and to the right of the car. He sat up and began picking stickers and gravel from his elbows and knees while we observed the stranger.

"That's a fancy set of binoculars, what do you suppose he's looking at?" I whispered.

Junebug apparently had removed all of the embedded objects and now devoted his full attention to the watcher.

"He's looking back at Mrs. Hardeman's."

"Yeah, but why?"

"I'll be dogged. He's watching Mrs. Duval."

"How do you know?"

"That's her room with the curtains open. I just saw her blonde hair...see there she is again."

"You're right, why's he watching her?"

"I don't know, let's just wait and see what happens."

The stranger continued his observation of the room until the front door of the boarding house slammed and Mrs. Duval walked out and to her Corvette, climbing in and roaring off with a squeal of her tires. She was followed a moment later by the Impala pulling away from the curb and heading in the same direction.

"Come on!" Junebug jumped up and started running down the street following the car.

We lost sight of it within a few blocks when it turned onto Gilmer Street, then turned again.

89

"Well, what now?" I asked while I was bent over trying to catch my breath.

"I guess we find something else to do while we wait for him to come back."

"Let's go see what Uncle Jasper's doing."

"All right, but don't mention the stranger until we get a chance to check him out a little more. If he isn't involved your uncle wouldn't ever let us live it down."

\*\*\*\*\*\*\*\*\*\*\*\*\*\*\*\*\*\*\*\*\*\*\*\*\*\*

We opened the door to the office and walked in, stopping abruptly as we saw a man standing in front of Uncle Jasper's desk shaking his hand.

"Boys, I'm glad y'all stopped by. Come on around here I've got somebody I want you to meet." My uncle waved us toward him. "Mr. Goldman, this is my nephew Joe Ben and his friend Junebug Walker."

The tubby man was dressed in a three piece suit and bow tie and was sweating like a stuck pig. He held out a pudgy hand adorned with a pinky ring glittering with diamonds and framed at the wrist end by a huge gold watch.

"Hello boys, glad to meet you."

We both shook hands and Junebug immediately wiped his on his pants, distaste at the feel of the man's sweaty palm outweighing what few good manners he possessed.

"This is the agent who handled Mr. Duval's books. He flew down from New York to check up on things."

"That's right. I want to thank you young fellows," he messed up Junebug's hair with his hand, earning a look from him that should have made the man glad Junebug wasn't any bigger than a pissant whose growth had been stunted, "for helping recover Ted's body. He was a great writer who didn't deserve to end up like that."

I just shrugged and kind of scuffed my shoes against the floor. Junebug kept looking at the man as if he was a three eyed Martian who'd just ate his dog.

"What can we do for you Mr. Goldman?" Uncle Jasper asked.

"Actually, I was hoping you would help me sort through Ted's things. His next book was due two weeks ago and the publisher is getting antsy. Pretty soon they're going to ask for their advance money back."

"Did he have his book finished?"

"I talked to him the day he disappeared and he said his rough draft was almost finished. He thought it would take another week at the most."

"Well, I'm afraid I won't be able to help you."

"Why not?"

"We've gone through his room and belongings thoroughly and haven't found a copy of any manuscript."

"You might not recognize it if you saw it. Ted was superstitious about his writing. The book would have been written in blue ink on yellow legal tablets. I imagine it would have been about 500 or so pages long."

"Sorry. There's nothing like that here." He reached into his desk drawer and withdrew the single typewritten sheet we'd found in the room and the legal pad that had been on the lawn chair at the "crime scene."

"These are the only things we found."

The agent picked up the pad and looked at it, then sat it down with a puzzled expression on his face.

"What's wrong?"

"This pad, it's Ted's handwriting, but it's just doodles and nonsense."

"So? A lot of people doodle while they're thinking."

"I know, but Ted was a fanatic about his writing. The only thing he'd write on these notepads were his books, he used white paper for everything else. Said it kept him focused and organized."

"Well, he might have forgot his other paper back at his room."

"Maybe. I guess anything's possible. But this typewritten page..."

"What about it?"

"He never typed his work until he was completely finished, plus, this book was behind schedule and he was going to send me his handwritten pages so I could have my secretary do the typing. I know he wasn't finished because he told me so right before he died. There's something just not right here."

"What was this book about?"

"Ted said he had investigated a bank robbery and murder from around here. The publisher liked the idea of a mystery writer really solving a twenty year old mystery and gave him a nice advance even though this was going to be his first non-fiction work."

"Did he say who did it?"

"No, I kept asking him but he said I could read it when the book was finished. He was afraid somebody would leak the secret and ruin sales."

"Mr. Goldberg, did you know Mr. Duval fairly well?"

"As well as anybody. I've represented him since he started writing, but we've never really been friends. I can't think of anybody you really could call his friend. He was kind of a recluse."

"Have you ever heard of anyone named Joshua Lomanto?"

He scratched his thinning hair for a moment. "No, I don't think so. Who is he?"

"He appears to be someone who was in a class Mr. Duval taught. We found a letter where Lomanto accuses him of stealing a book he wrote and publishing it under Duval's name."

"Which book?"

"Apparently it was called Mystery Train."

"That hasn't even been published yet. It was due out last week, but got delayed for a few months. As a matter of fact, the book was originally called 'Death on the Rails', the publishing company hasn't even released the new name to the public."

"How would this Lomanto know the name then?"

"Beats me. He may work for the publisher or have an inside source. If you really wanted to find out something like that it probably wouldn't be too hard."

"What can you tell me about his marriage?"

"You mean Julia? That was a strange arrangement, but one he was satisfied with until recently."

"What happened?"

"I don't know. A couple of months ago he asked me for the name of my attorney, said he'd been thinking about going ahead and cutting the ties with Julia once and for all. He never mentioned it again and I never asked. Say, I read an article that said Julia was one of the suspects. Do you really think she did it?"

"I haven't excluded her yet."

"She never struck me as that type, but I guess you never know." He stood and shook Uncle Jasper's hand, then reached out to ruffle Junebug's hair, missing as he dodged out of reach and glared. "Well, I guess I'd better be going. Call me if you find that manuscript...or if I can be of any help."

# CHAPTER 11

Rather than walking around hoping we ran into the stranger we'd been watching Junebug decided it would be more productive to conduct a "stake out".

"What's that?" I asked when he first suggested the idea.

"It's where we hide someplace and watch the house until he shows up, then we watch and see what he does."

"Why do they call it a stake out?"

"I don't know, it's some kind of police code I guess, now do you want to help or not?"

"It sounds boring."

"Naw, it'll be like real police work. Just think how famous we'll be if this guy turns out to be the real murderer and we're the ones who catch him, won't that be something?"

"I guess. Okay, I'll try it for a while."

We made a detour through Aunt Sarah's kitchen and fixed a sack of food to take with us. I cut some thick slabs from a smoked ham she had in the refrigerator while Junebug made up some of his awful sandwiches. On one slice of white bread he'd smear mustard and on the other a thick layer of peanut butter, then he'd take a big slab of onion and put in between there. The only thing that made me gag worse than those concoctions was watching Uncle Jasper take a slice of corn bread and crumble it up into a glass of buttermilk, then consume the whole mess smacking his lips happily the whole time. Those two could eat stuff that'd make a buzzard puke.

Junebug insisted on taking up the same vantage point as before, huddled down behind the hedges in

Miss Pearlie Robinson's yard. We'd no sooner gotten settled in good than Mrs. Duval's blue Corvette came roaring down the street and turned into the driveway beside the boarding house. Sure enough, a few minutes later the Impala pulled up to the same spot on the curb as before and shut off its engine. The man raised the same binoculars and began watching again.

Time passed very slowly as we sweated in the hot sun, watching the man watch Mrs. Duval. Occasionally I could see him look at his watch and write on a notebook mounted on his dashboard.

I opened the sack of food and passed one of Junebug's sandwiches to him, which he immediately began eating, munching happily. There was something about the odor of peanut butter, onion, and mustard that caused me to lose my appetite so I folded my ham sandwich back up in the waxed paper and put it back into the sack.

Junebug saw me and offered a bite of his meal, sticking the stinking mess up under my nose, which I wrinkled up as I shook my head and held my breath until he pulled it away with a shrug of his shoulders.

After a few more minutes I felt him twitching next to me.

"Be still Junebug."

"Mmmph unnngh," he said around a mouthful of peanut butter and onion.

I ignored him until he started fidgeting again.

"Junebug, be still. He's gonna notice the bushes shaking if you don't quit."

"MMMPH UNNNGH," he said louder and began wiggling even more.

"I said quit it. He's gonna hear you."

Suddenly Junebug jumped up and started beating at his crotch area, hopping around and babbling incoherently. I was so surprised by his actions I forgot about the stranger we were watching until I heard a voice behind me.

95

"What's the matter with your friend?"

I jumped in surprise, then sputtered out, "I...I...I...don't know. We were playing and he all of a sudden started acting like that."

"Does he ever have fits?"

"Just when he gets mad."

"No, I mean like epileptic fits?"

"Oh, no, nothing like that."

By this time Junebug was laying on the ground and clawing frantically at his belt, eventually undoing it and kicking his shorts off. Just as he did I saw a small green grass snake, obviously the source of his discomfort, slither out the bottom of his pants leg and into the lawn.

He stood up, red in the face, and quickly put his breeches back on.

"Are you all right?", the stranger asked.

"Lnngh...", he stopped trying to talk and took a moment to swallow the rest of the peanut butter in his mouth.

"I'm fine, now that I'm not sharing my clothes with anything else."

"Well, okay. You boys be careful and stay out of trouble." The man shook his head and headed across the street to the boarding house.

We stood there and watched until he was inside, then in unspoken agreement headed toward my house.

I stayed quiet for a few blocks but eventually couldn't resist commenting.

"You know, I don't remember the Hardy Boys ever having their investigation interrupted by a snake crawling into their drawers."

"Shut up," he said sullenly.

"Yes sir, screaming at the top of your lungs and dropping your pants in front of a suspect is probably the least likely way to get noticed I've ever heard of."

"Shut up."

"The only thing that would have made it better would have been if you'd run around a little bit without your pants, rather than getting right back up and putting them on."

"Shut up."

"I do believe you have got an incredible future ahead of you as a private investigator, Junebug. I mean, with your sophisticated surveillance techniques and impressive ability to remain unnoticed I bet you make a million dollars solving all sorts of mysteries."

"Shut up."

Uncle Jasper was sure gonna get a kick out of this.

\*\*\*\*\*\*\*\*\*\*\*\*\*\*\*\*\*\*\*\*\*\*\*\*

"So what do we do now?" I asked while we were sitting on the porch entertaining ourselves by watching Jake drag himself around the back yard, pulling with his front legs and scratching his rump on the ground.

Uncle Jasper had driven over to Sumter to talk with the medical examiner in person but hadn't let us go with him. He said we'd had enough excitement for one day and besides, he'd be too embarrassed if Junebug suddenly decided to strip naked in front of Dr. Everett.

I thought his remark was kind of funny, but Junebug sulled up and wouldn't talk to me for a good half hour, although apparently he wasn't mad enough to go home.

"I still think we ought to find out who that man is and what he's doing in St. John." Apparently he'd decided I'd been punished enough and was now talking to me again.

"How do we do that? I'm pretty sure he'll recognize us if he sees us again." I started to make another comment about our earlier stakeout, but changed my mind. If Junebug got too mad he'd just go find Danielle and I'd have to hunt for somebody to hang around with. Since Junebug had become my best friend most of the other boys in town had become a little leery of keeping company with me. I guess either them or their parents were afraid he'd rub off on me.

"Let's go and take a look in his car. Maybe there's a clue in there we could use."

"I don't think that's a good idea. I'm pretty sure Uncle Jasper wouldn't want us digging through somebody else's property."

"I swear Joe Ben, you're turning into a sissy."

"I am not, I'm just using my head. The last time you had a brilliant idea we ended up finding a body. Who knows what could happen this time."

"Are you gonna help me or not?"

"Not this time. If I got caught I'd be grounded the rest of the summer."

"Well I can't do it by myself."

"Then you just can't do it."

"Sometimes you make me so mad. I guess I'll have to go get Danielle to help me."

I'm sure he intended that to goad me into giving in, but all it did was make me mad.

"That's fine, you go get her. I'm beginning to think you'd rather play with a girl anyway."

"You're just jealous because she likes me."

"Am not."

"Are too."

"Am not. Anyways, who'd want a gotch-eyed girl hanging around them all the time?"

I was sorry as soon as I'd said it. Junebug got an awful expression on his face that I'd never seen before and just stared at me, then ran down the steps and toward his house. I yelled at him to stop, but either he didn't hear me or was ignoring me.

The day had started out crummy and gotten worse.

\*\*\*\*\*\*\*\*\*\*\*\*\*\*\*\*\*\*\*\*\*\*\*\*\*\*\*\*

98

I moped around the house the rest of that afternoon trying to find something to do. None of my books held my interest for long and I finished the only model car I had left, a Red Baron that looked just like one of my Hot Wheels.

Eventually Aunt Sarah shooed me out of her way and into the back yard, where I sat in the tire swing until Uncle Jasper drove up.

"You look like you lost your best friend," he said as he got out of the car.

"I think I did."

"Something happen between you and Junebug?"

"We had an argument."

"Where is he?"

"He left in a huff a couple of hours ago. I think he was going to see Danielle."

"Well, don't worry, he'll be back."

We started walking toward the house. Just as we got to the back steps I heard steps running up the gravel driveway and turned, expecting to see Junebug. Instead it was Danielle running as fast as she could in a dress and her patent leather shoes.

"Come quick," she gasped out. "Junebug's been kidnapped."

\*\*\*\*\*\*\*\*\*\*\*\*\*\*\*\*\*\*\*\*\*\*\*\*\*\*\*\*

"What?"

"Hurry! Hurry! Junebug's been kidnapped."

"What happened?" Uncle Jasper asked.

"I was helping Junebug investigate and the next thing I knew the car was driving off."

"Slow up. What car? What are you talking about?"

"He wanted to look inside of a suspect's car and asked me to keep a watch for the owner. The car was parked in front of Mrs. Hardeman's place and he crawled in through the window. A few minutes later Janet came by in her new dress and stopped to talk.

Before I realized it the man climbed into his car and drove away."

"Who was the man?"

"He was somebody Junebug saw down at the cafe today. He got the idea this guy was a suspect and...well, you know how Junebug is," I volunteered.

He nodded his head. "Do you know what he looked like?

"Well, actually we were on a stake out and watched him for quite a while earlier today."

"A stake out? Exactly what were you looking for?"

"I don't know. Anything suspicious I guess."

"Would you recognize him if you saw him again?"

"Yes sir. I'd recognize the car too."

Uncle Jasper turned his attention back to Danielle. "Which way did the car go?"

"I saw it turn onto Green Street and head back toward Main, but I didn't see where it went after that."

"Are you sure he was still in the car?"

"Yes, I'm sure. There wasn't anyplace else he could have gone."

"You run on home now and don't worry. I'll make sure Junebug is safe and sound."

She turned and left, still sniffling.

"That's the problem with separating you two, together you equal about a lick of sense but apart there isn't any hope." He turned and opened the door to the patrol car. "Well, get in. I sure can't leave you here by yourself. There's no telling what kind of dramatic rescue you'd try to pull."

I climbed in and Uncle Jasper spun the tires when we left the driveway. He was keeping a calm appearance but I could tell he was a little concerned, although I wasn't sure if it was for Junebug or the stranger.

A drive around town didn't reveal the whereabouts of the Impala or the driver, and definitely no sign of Junebug. We covered the streets in a methodical fashion driving up one and down the other. I got more worried with each passing minute and started blaming myself. If I'd have been with Junebug I would have kept a better watch than Danielle and he wouldn't be in this trouble.

"He doesn't seem to be in town. Why don't we take a run out to Sandy Creek and if we don't see anything between here and there we'll call in an all points bulletin to the State Police. This isn't exactly a kidnapping but I think they'd forgive me for calling it that in light of the situation."

The road out to the creek was nearly deserted. About a half a mile before our turn off Uncle Jasper pulled the car up next to a tractor driving down the road and motioned for me to roll down the window.

"Howdy Bert."

Bert Lansing was a farmer in the area who grew corn, a little of which he sold, a little of which he kept to feed his hogs but the majority of which he was rumored to turn into a liquid crop which had a ready market in Northeast Texas. Uncle Jasper and him were constantly looking out for each other, him so his still wouldn't be found and Uncle Jasper so he could find it.

"Howdy Jasper, howdy Joe Ben. What brings you out in this heat? Thinking about still hunting today?"

"Too hot for that. Actually we're looking for a brown Impala that may have passed this way."

"As a matter of fact I saw a brown car turn down the road next to the creek about a half hour ago while I was plowing."

"Thanks Ben, drop by and drink a cup of coffee at the office next time you're in town."

"No thanks. Jails make me nervous, I'll let you buy me a piece of pie next time I see you at Doc's though."

Uncle Jasper waved and pulled away, turning right onto the dusty path just after we crossed over the creek. He drove a short way down the road paralleling the creek then pulled off on a side track and parked behind a thicket where the patrol car couldn't be seen.

"Come on and keep quiet." He motioned for me to follow him across the road and into the trees between it and the creek.

We slowly made our way through the trees in the direction away from the highway, keeping an eye out for the Impala. I spotted it just as we were getting close to where we'd found Mr. Duval's lawn chair and belongings.

The car was parked in nearly the same place Uncle Jasper had parked the patrol car the day we'd found the body. My uncle must have seen it about the same time since I felt his hand on my shoulder and looked around to see him hold a finger to his lips signaling me to be quiet.

It was then I realized Uncle Jasper wasn't carrying his gun. I knew he usually didn't but was beginning to wonder if I'd taken Junebug's suspicions about the contents of the violin case too lightly.

We crept slowly toward the car, stopping every few feet to look carefully in all directions. The woods were still. Where normally would be the sounds of birds or the whirring of cicadas fooled by the shadowy interior into believing nightfall was near, there was only silence. This eerie quiet was probably no more than would be usual when humans crept through their domain, but the animal and insect kingdom's lack of expression made the whole scene more ominous.

We got down on our hands and knees to advance to the car, in case the stranger was huddled down in his seat. Uncle Jasper poked his head up and peered into the interior of the car then stood to full height.

"It's empty."

He carefully opened the door, slowly so as to not create any more noise than was necessary. On the front seat was a box of papers, sitting on top of which was the violin case Junebug had seen. I reached around Uncle Jasper and tried to flip the latch, but it was locked. On the rear floorboard was a blanket that may have provided Junebug some cover in his ride.

"Where's he at?" I asked.

"I don't know, but he isn't here. I'm going to take a look by the creek," he looked at me. "Maybe you'd better wait back at the car. I don't know what's going on here but it's mighty peculiar."

"If you don't mind I'd just as soon stay with you. The idea of waiting by myself isn't particularly appealing."

"All right, just stick close."

"Don't worry about that."

We reentered the woods and walked toward the creek, just to the side of the path leading to the small clearing where we'd found the writer's things. As we approached the glade I felt a small chill run up my spine when I thought about the fact that this was the last place Ted Duval had spent any time while alive. His next stop after here was the waters of Sandy Creek, where he waited for Junebug and me to find him.

It was these morbid thoughts and the memory of Duval's corpse which were running through my mind when I heard a noise and felt myself grabbed from behind.

# CHAPTER 12

I tried to scream but only managed a weak gasp.
Uncle Jasper must have been surprised as well since he
jumped forward about two feet.

"What are y'all doing out here?" Junebug
whispered in my ear.

I yanked out of his grasp and turned to face him.
"Are you crazy? You liked to've scared me to death."

He grinned at me. "Sorry."

I could tell he wasn't sorry at all.

"Boy, I might have put a bullet into you. Don't
you have any sense at all?"

"That's funny Sheriff. It'd be mighty hard to
shoot anybody without your gun, wouldn't it?"

Uncle Jasper just looked exasperated.

"What are y'all creeping through the woods
for?" Junebug asked.

"We were looking for you, Danielle said you'd
been kidnapped."

"Isn't that just like a girl? First she doesn't keep
a lookout and then she gets you and the sheriff all in a
tizzy for nothing. I can take care of myself."

"What happened?" Uncle Jasper asked.

"I was looking for clues in the man's car when I
heard him crossing the street so I covered up with a
blanket and laid on the back floorboard. When he
stopped here I waited a few minutes after I heard the
door close and then got out. I looked up the creek that
way," he pointed toward the highway, "but didn't see
him so I thought I'd check the other way. That's when I
saw you two sneaking around the woods."

"Who is he?" I was curious exactly how much
Junebug had managed to achieve without me.

"I don't know. I saw some papers but didn't have time to look through them."

"Anything else?"

"A whole bunch of camera stuff and enough junk food to keep an army alive for a week." He looked thoughtful for a moment. "The Twinkies were a little stale though. I could only eat two packages."

"Why don't we go see if we can find out what's going on? You two follow me and be careful. If I hold my hand up you stop immediately."

When we had nodded to indicate we understood Uncle Jasper started back down the path toward the creek. Just as we got close Uncle Jasper motioned for us to squat down behind a clump of cane plants growing to one side of the trail. It was barely big enough for all three of us, but was bushy enough to provide a pretty good hiding place.

A splashing from the direction of the creek indicated the reason for my uncle's concern and our concealment.

The stranger, pants dripping wet and water squishing in his shoes, made his way down the path headed toward his car. Every few feet he would turn and point a camera around his neck back in the direction of the creek and shoot a few pictures. He spent a couple of minutes at the clearing snapping photographs before continuing toward the Impala, fooling with his camera.

Uncle Jasper reached down and picked up a stick from the ground then stood up.

"When I get out of sight you boys count to a hundred, then head toward the car slowly and quietly." He looked at Junebug, then added, "And count slowly. If I see you or hear you any earlier than that I'm going to find me a limb as big around as my arm and whale the tar out of you. Got it?"

Junebug's eyes bugged out till I thought they'd pop. He didn't say a word, just nodded his head emphatically.

"If something happens to me y'all head through the woods to the highway and find Bert, then get him to call the state police."

With that he stepped out from behind the stand of cane and carefully followed the stranger's trail.

I began counting when Uncle Jasper disappeared around a curve. When I reached 75 I leaned down and whispered to Junebug.

"I think that's long enough. Let's go."

He shook his head. I could see his lips moving as he counted to himself.

I counted to 25, then said, "All right. That's a hundred, let's go."

"Shut up Joe Ben. Your uncle sounded serious. I'm going to count to two hundred just to be sure."

Eventually he was satisfied he'd waited long enough to avoid the whipping Uncle Jasper had promised and we began making our way through the trees in the direction taken by the stranger and Uncle Jasper.

\*\*\*\*\*\*\*\*\*\*\*\*\*\*\*\*\*\*\*\*\*\*\*\*\*\*

"Now why should I believe you?"

I heard my Uncle Jasper's voice asking as we came into sight of the car.

"Because it's the truth. Look, my I.D. card is in my wallet, take a look at it."

The man was leaning over the car with his legs wide apart and his hands on the hood. Uncle Jasper was standing behind him with the stick stuck in his back.

"I'll get around to that. Now don't make any sudden moves, this gun has got a hair trigger and I'd hate for it to go off accidentally." He poked the stick harder to emphasize his point.

"I'm not moving, just be careful, okay?"

"Joe Ben, can you hear me?" my uncle yelled.

"Yes sir."

"Run to the car and get my handcuffs out of the glove compartment."

"Yes sir."

I took off at a run, Junebug right next to me. The car wasn't that far away and we were back quickly, even though Junebug and I had a brief tussle over who got to carry the shiny, stainless steel implements.

I handed them to Uncle Jasper.

"All right stranger. Very slowly put your right hand behind your back."

The handcuff was clicked around the right wrist with one hand, the other continuing to hold the stick pressed into his back.

"Now the left hand."

The man leaned over and placed his chest on the hood, sticking his left arm behind him. A moment later a metallic "snick" indicated both hands were now restrained.

Uncle Jasper reached forward and pulled the man upright by the collar of his shirt, then turned him around to face him.

"Where's your wallet?"

"On the seat under my notebook. Say, where's your gun?"

Uncle Jasper dropped the stick and opened the car door, moving the man around to where he wouldn't be able to slam it on him if he was of a mind to.

"Left it at home. I can't shoot a pistol worth a darn anyway."

He picked through the wallet for a while, finally extracting two laminated items.

"Well, it appears you told the truth about your name anyway. And this other card does state Mr. Nathan Bailey works for Trans-National Insurance."

"Will you let me go now?"

"Not quite yet. Why don't we take a ride into town so I can verify all of this. If you check out and can offer me a reasonable explanation as to what you were doing I'll think about releasing you."

He shut the door and took him by the arm.

"Come on boys, let's give Mr. Bailey here a ride into St. John and show him how hospitable we are to strangers."

\*\*\*\*\*\*\*\*\*\*\*\*\*\*\*\*\*\*\*\*\*\*

Junebug had placed a chair outside the cell door and spent the time glaring at the man, occasionally firing off a question which was ignored by the prisoner.

Within an hour Uncle Jasper had his answers and let Nathan Bailey out of the lone cell which served as St. John's jail.

"All right Mr. Bailey, I apologize for the inconvenience but I had to be sure you were telling the truth."

"That's all right Sheriff. It's not the first time I've been in jail, although the deputies are usually a little bigger." He indicated Junebug who was apparently unimpressed with Uncle Jasper's pronouncement of Bailey's innocence and was still glaring.

"What brings you to St. John, Mr. Bailey?"

"I'm investigating a case for Trans-National. They carried a policy on Ted Duval and have some concerns about his death. I understand it's still being investigated?"

"Yep. We've got a bunch of suspects but nothing definitive. What were you hoping to find out at the creek?"

"Sheriff, we've found that in cases in small towns the investigation isn't always conducted in a.....methodical way."

"You mean us country boys don't know what we're doing."

Mr. Bailey looked embarrassed. "I didn't mean that. What I meant was the latest techniques take a while to make it out of the cities into rural areas. That's where I come in. The insurance company sends me to classes throughout the year so I can keep up with the latest advances and kind of look things over and make sure you haven't missed anything."

"You must have missed the one where they taught you how to tell the difference between a stick and a pistol when it's poking you in the back, huh?" Junebug chimed in.

"Yeah...well...I guess you can't learn everything."

"Exactly what are you investigating?" Uncle Jasper asked.

"Our insurance policy carries a double indemnity clause in the event someone meets their death by something other than natural means."

"What's the policy worth?"

"Its face value is $ 250,000.00, but if it really was a murder it means the beneficiary will receive a half a million tax free dollars."

"Who was named as the beneficiary?"

"His wife, Julia Duval."

# CHAPTER 13

"That's all right Sheriff, you're just doing your job," Julia Duval said as she unpacked the bag Uncle Jasper had let her fill before he took her down to the jail.

"We'll try to make your stay here just as comfortable as we can, but you need to understand that you're a prisoner, not a guest. There's going to be a certain amount of discomfort that comes with that."

I still thought she was innocent and told him so, but Uncle Jasper had arrested her anyway.

"Nobody as pretty as her could be a murderer, I just know it," I'd said.

At least he'd let me say my piece and hadn't laughed. Junebug, however, hadn't been as polite.

"Too pretty to be a murderer," he'd gasped in between guffaws. "Joe Ben, how naive can you get?"

"Shut up Junebug. At least I didn't get kidnapped by an insurance adjuster who plays the fiddle for a hobby."

He straightened up.

"That was different."

Mrs. Duval had taken being arrested without much excitement. She hadn't broken down in tears, or raised her voice, or shown any real emotion at all. To be honest, she hadn't even acted surprised.

Even Uncle Jasper remarked on it.

"You don't act worried."

"I'm not. I told you I didn't kill my husband."

Uncle Jasper just shrugged his shoulders and flopped down in his chair, putting his feet up on the desk and opening his paper. I watched Junebug wander into the back room, followed shortly by the sound of

110

the Dialing for Dollars afternoon movie coming on the television set back there.

I sat down on the stool in front of the cell and watched the blonde woman unpack. Soon she finished and took a seat on the cot in front of me.

"What's wrong Joe Ben?"

"Nothing." I looked down at my hands.

"Come on now. If there is one thing I know, it's when a man is down in the dumps." She reached through the bars and smoothed the hair back from my forehead. "Now tell me what's the matter?"

"I didn't think you were the one."

"The one what?"

"The one who killed him. I thought you were innocent."

"Joe Ben, I am innocent."

"Do you promise?"

She put her hand under my chin and lifted my head until I looked into her eyes.

"I promise. Joe Ben, before this is all over everyone in town will know I didn't kill my husband."

# CHAPTER 14

Mrs. Duval's trial was even more of a "to do" than her husband's funeral had been. Within a few days of her arrest reporters were once again scrambling around town trying to dig up new and exciting facts to set their stories apart from the others.

The jail was the focus of much of the attention as reporters were constantly in and out of the office, either taking pictures of the surroundings or the prisoner. Despite repeated requests, she continued to deny interviews.

Eventually Uncle Jasper had tired of all of the traffic and hoopla and officially closed his office to the public. I think it was because every time he got ready to put his feet up on the desk and take a nap he was interrupted. Even me and Junebug were banned from the premises except for delivering messages and such. This was probably due to the "official" tours Junebug had paraded through the office one too many times.

I was there delivering Uncle Jasper's lunch one day when a knock sounded on the door and Cecil waddled over to open it.

"What can I do for you?" he asked the unseen visitor.

"You can let me in out of this heat for starters," a raspy voice said from outside the door.

"Oh no," Uncle Jasper muttered to himself.

A man dressed in a light blue and white cotton suit stepped through the door. He was carrying a cane and a briefcase and perched on top of his head was a big, round straw hat with a red bandanna tied around it.

"Howdy Jasper. Long time no see." The man walked over to in front of my uncle's desk and set his things down, then removed his hat and mopped a shiny, bald head with a handkerchief he pulled from his pocket.

"I'd heard you retired," Uncle Jasper said.

"Not hardly. I can't rest as long as people are being falsely accused and their constitutional rights are being violated. It's just not the Christian thing to do."

Uncle Jasper snorted. "Since when did you become such a church going, religious fellow?"

"Now Jasper you know I've always had a disposition toward the scriptures."

"Quoting them, yes. It's the living them you've had a problem with."

The man reached down and mussed my hair with a liver spotted hand. "And who is this fine, upstanding young gentleman?"

"This is my nephew, Joe Ben. Joe Ben, this is Percival Proctor, the meanest, sneakiest, most ornery human Baldwin County has ever had the misfortune of producing. He's also a lawyer."

He grasped my hand and shook it firmly.

"Pleased to meet you," I mumbled.

"Jasper, why do you always insist on saying such hateful things about me? Not still sore over that moonshine are you?"

"Of course not. Although you know good and well that was white lightning we seized."

"Then how come it was water in the bottles you brought to court?"

"Because you switched them somehow."

"Are you accusing me of unethical conduct?"

"Percy, you wouldn't know an ethic if it came up and bit you right on the butt. I bet you don't even know what ethics are."

"Sure I do. Ethics are what cause you to lose cases."

Uncle Jasper just sat there, red in the face and fuming.

"Enough small talk now Jasper, I'm here to see my client."

"Who?"

"My client, Julia Duval. You remember her don't you? The lovely lady you have wrongfully accused of a heinous crime."

"I know who Julia Duval is, I just didn't know she was your client."

Uncle Jasper got up and walked over to the cell, staring fiercely at Mrs. Duval, who just stood and looked back with a slight smile on her face.

"Y'all can talk through the bars," he said.

"I know how much you like my company, but do you think it would be possible for us to have a wee bit more privacy?" the lawyer asked.

"You can use that back office, but I'll have to handcuff her while she's out of her cell," Uncle Jasper said.

"Jasper Johnson, surely you're not afraid of this pitiful waif."

"Sheriff, I promise I'll be good," Mrs. Duval pleaded.

"Well, all right. But it's because you haven't asked for any favors or caused any trouble, not because of anything he's done," Uncle Jasper indicated Percy Proctor by jerking his head in his direction.

He unlocked the cell door and watched as the two walked into the back room and carefully shut the door behind them.

"Uncle Jasper, your sweet potatoes are gonna get cold if you don't eat 'em pretty quick," I reminded him of the lunch sitting on his desk.

"I believe I've lost my appetite."

\*\*\*\*\*\*\*\*\*\*\*\*\*\*\*\*\*\*\*\*\*\*\*\*

Normally the trial itself would have been held over in Sumter, the county seat, but a fire the year before had decimated the courthouse and construction had not started on a new one. Judge Lawton Bundy had released the news that instead the trial would be held right here in St. John, in the Bijou movie house. The theater had originally been used for vaudeville and other live productions and had a large stage over which they'd mounted the movie screen. Three tables and chairs had been set up for the judge and lawyers, Judge Bundy's rising above the others by virtue of being located atop some packing crates obtained from over at the shingle factory.

The jury box consisted of twelve chairs arranged in two rows to one side. This left three hundred seats or so, not counting the balcony, in the actual theater to be used by the spectators.

Me and Junebug watched the men setting up the "courtroom" one day. For some reason, Junebug had taken an instant liking to Percy Proctor, possibly because their personalities were so much alike. He'd also taken to wearing a white straw hat that faintly resembled Mr. Proctor's. I thought it made him look like a deranged Huckleberry Finn.

"You know Joe Ben," he said to me while we were watching the men work, "I'm beginning to agree with you. I think Mrs. Duval is innocent."

"What changed your mind?"

"Listening to Mr. Proctor argue with your uncle every other day. Based on my experience, I think the case is shaky."

"Your experience? Junebug, there you go again. You don't have any more experience with this kind of thing than Jake does."

"That's not true. Didn't I watch the whole Lester Boggs trial two years ago?"

"Yeah, but Lester Boggs stole a cow, he didn't murder anybody."

"Well, it's still the legal process isn't it? I've seen every Perry Mason episode twice and watch Dragnet every time I get a chance. Plus, I've read every one of

115

the Hardy Boys mysteries. That ought to count for something."

"It does. It explains why you start acting so foolish every time you get excited. This isn't TV or a book, this is real life. They're not the same."

"Well, it still means I've got some experience."

There wasn't any use arguing when he got like this. Junebug was stubborn as a mule when he got his mind set on something.

"So what does your vast amount of experience tell you we need to do?" I asked.

He ignored the sarcasm. "The answer is obvious. The only way we can prove she's innocent is by proving who is really guilty. We need to figure out who robbed the bank."

"What are you talking about?"

"The only suspects we have are Mrs. Duval, that guy who wrote the letter to Mr. Duval..."

"Lomanto," I interrupted.

"Whatever....and whoever broke into Duval's room and stole the book he was writing. The only ones who would go to all that trouble would be someone actually involved in the robbery so..." He looked at me expectantly. When I didn't say anything he sighed and continued.

"So if we solve the robbery we know who stole the book and also who killed Duval. Doesn't that make sense?"

"What about Lomanto?"

"Do you know where to find him, or even where to start looking?"

"No."

"Neither do I. But we do know where to start investigating the robbery don't we?"

In some strange way Junebug was making sense. The fact that I thought so worried me, since each time he'd convinced me he was right in the past I'd ended up involved in something I'd later regret.

116

"No, where?"

"In your uncle's office."

That was logical. We watched until the workmen had finished the jury box, then left to begin our quest.

*************************

"What makes you think you can solve a twenty year old robbery that baffled the F.B.I.?" Uncle Jasper asked when I announced our plan.

"They didn't have my secret weapon...Junebug Walker."

Junebug beamed at my uncle, who just stared and then walked to the back room, returning shortly with a manila folder crammed with papers.

"Good luck to y'all. If you figure it out, let me know so I can drive you to wherever you need to go and make the arrests." He walked back to his desk chuckling to himself.

Junebug watched him leave then leaned over to me.

"Do you think he was serious?"

"No Junebug, he was just picking at us."

He sat down, apparently satisfied.

"That's good, because I'm not planning on us sharing the glory with anybody if we've done all the work."

That was my friend, so confident he'd go bear hunting with a slingshot, fearless enough to fight a rattlesnake and spot him the first two bites.

"Look here Joe Ben," Junebug said after we'd been looking through the papers for a while. "These are the witness reports. None of them ever heard the men say anything to each other. Do you know what that means?"

I shook my head.

"It means they had a plan already worked out. They knew where everything was and how the bank operated. I bet the bank robbers were from right around here. That'd explain why they found the car here, the men had another one stashed."

"But here's a picture of the car...look at the license plate."

He leaned over and peered at the black and white picture in which the word South Carolina could clearly be read on the license plate.

"Aw, that don't mean anything. They just went out of state to steal a car and use in their getaway."

"They went all the way to South Carolina just to steal a car?"

"Sure, who'd ever think anybody would do something like that? It was just a trick to throw the law off track."

"Pretty complicated trick."

"It worked didn't it?"

Who could argue with logic like that?

We looked through the file for the rest of the day, but didn't make any dramatic breakthroughs in the case, although occasionally Junebug would snap his fingers and get all excited as he found some new piece of evidence, only to read a few more pages and find the lead had been tracked down and discarded when it didn't pan out.

"Maybe we're going at this all wrong," Junebug said as we walked toward my house. Uncle Jasper had chased us out of the office when he left to make his daily drive through town. Cecil remained there to keep an eye on Mrs. Duval but he made us leave anyway.

"Junebug makes him nervous," was all my uncle said when we protested at being ejected.

The walk home was actually a welcome change after being cooped up all afternoon looking through the papers.

"What do you mean?" I asked.

"Maybe we should look around town and figure out who might have done the robbery, then look to see if the evidence fits."

"How do we do that?"

"We can start by eliminating everybody under about 40, since they'd have been too young to drive and not likely suspects."

"That makes sense."

"We can also eliminate all the women, since none of the reports say anything about any of the robbers being female. They also don't say anything about any of them being black so that would narrow it down some more."

"That still leaves a bunch of people."

"Yeah, but a lot of them haven't ever had two nickels to rub together. The robbers would have had a load of money, so we could begin by looking at the men who have at least a little bit of money."

"How many does that leave?"

He sighed. "A bunch, but at least it's a start. I'll tell you what, why don't we go over to the bank and snoop around? It hasn't changed much since the fifties, maybe we'll spot something that gives us a clue."

It sounded as good as anything I'd thought of.

We entered the bank through the revolving glass door. Junebug went in first and got about halfway around when the door kind of stuck.

"Push Joe Ben." His voice sounded kind of muffled through the glass.

I shoved as hard as I could. Junebug was pushing so hard I could see the muscles in his scrawny legs knotting up.

"Harder!"

"I'm pushing as hard as I can, you push harder."

"I'll bust a gut if I push any harder," he said. "Let me think for a minute."

You'd think someone in the bank would have noticed our plight and offered to help, but apparently kids being stuck in the door was a common occurrence.

"All right. Joe Ben, you back up and get a running start. Hit the door with your shoulder as hard as you can."

"I don't know if that's such a good idea, what if..."

He interrupted me. "Joe Ben, I've gotta pee. Hurry up."

I shrugged my shoulders and backed up a few paces, then lowered my head and ran toward the door like Jim Brown busting through the defensive line on the way to a touchdown.

I hit the door hard enough to cause my shoulder to go numb, but the force knocked it to spinning and Junebug shot out the other side and into the lobby, colliding with Hiram Gillespie who had unwisely chosen that moment to see what the commotion from the front was all about. Junebug hit him at just under the speed of sound, both of them sliding across the floor until they were stopped by the counter where people were filling out their deposit slips.

"Get up! You're crushing my hat! Get up!" Junebug was furiously tugging on the edge of his hat which was poking out from under Mr. Gillespie.

\*\*\*\*\*\*\*\*\*\*\*\*\*\*\*\*\*\*\*\*\*\*\*\*\*

"Junebug, they threw us out because you knocked the president of the bank on his butt."

"How could I have known he was gonna walk in front of the door right then? If he'd have stayed out of the way none of this would have ever happened."

"I really don't think it was his fault."

"If he'd have been looking where he was going he could have missed me. He was probably just in a hurry to throw some widows and orphans out of their house or something."

"I don't think he would have got as upset if you hadn't kicked him so hard."

"HE WAS SITTING ON MY HAT! I asked him to get off two or three times but he wouldn't listen."

"I think he was dazed Junebug, you hit him like you'd been shot out of a cannon."

"He heard me good enough after I kicked him a couple of times."

"I guess that ends our snooping around the bank. We'll be lucky if old man Gillespie doesn't have the bank guard try to shoot us if we walk past on the sidewalk."

"Oh, he's just an old grouch. He's had it in for me for years."

"You know, some people would say you started it. That was the cat that his wife had won all those blue ribbons with."

"I don't know why everybody just assumes I had anything to do with it. Besides, I glued...I mean, somebody glued all the hair back on it before they brought it home."

A voice interrupted our conversation as we strolled down the street.

"Hey boys how've y'all been?"

We both turned to look toward the speaker.

"Hi Mr. Edwards, how're you?"

Mr. Edwards was one of the first reporters to arrive in St. John after we'd found the body. He was from up in Oklahoma and treated us more like people than little kids. He was so nice Junebug hadn't even charged him for the tour or the lecture.

"Just fine. You wouldn't have anything new to report would you?"

"No, not really. But to be honest with you, Uncle Jasper said he'd skin us alive if we discussed the case with anyone before the trial was over."

"I understand. I certainly wouldn't want to get you in any trouble. Do you know of any other angles that might be interesting?"

"Me and Joe Ben are investigating the bank robbery," Junebug piped in.

"Is that right? Do you mean the same one Duval was writing his book about?"

"Yep."

"That might make an interesting story, especially since you two were the ones who found Duval's corpse in the first place." He got out of the car and leaned back against the hood, then spent the next ten minutes asking us questions. From the way Junebug answered you'd have sworn our next step was to announce our findings and arrest the robbers.

After Mr. Edwards ran out of questions he reached through the window of the car and pulled out one of those big, fancy cameras and took a bunch of pictures of me and Junebug in various poses.

"Is this gonna be in the newspaper?" I asked him.

"It might. I like the concept and think a lot of other people will too. You boys are certainly newsworthy. There are not a lot of twelve year olds who have had as interesting a summer as you have."

"Isn't that the truth?" I responded.

We talked for a few minutes more before Mr. Edwards excused himself and drove off.

Junebug stood on the sidewalk and watched him leave, then turned to me grinning from ear to ear.

"I told you. Stick with me and I'll make you famous."

# CHAPTER 15

The anxiously awaited day of trial was soon upon us. The elite of St. John turned out in all their finery, dressed more appropriately for a formal dinner than a murder trial. Seated front row center were Mayor Quinton and his wife, with the members of the city council taking the remainder of the premier seats. The auditorium was soon filled with other people from around the county, as well as reporters from across the country. Bearded New Yorkers fought for elbow room with sharecroppers, each equally enthralled by the spectacle which was about to unfold.

Uncle Jasper and Aunt Sarah were on the second row. After much pleading and begging, they'd agreed Junebug and I could sit with them, with the stern warning of dire consequences should we misbehave. To ensure we maintained a proper level of decorum Uncle Jasper placed Junebug between him and Aunt Sarah and banished me to the other side of her.

Aunt Sarah was wearing her finest Sunday dress along with a new hat she'd bought down in Tyler the week before. Uncle Jasper shifted uncomfortably and continually tugged at the starched collar of his shirt. He wore the only suit he possessed, the one normally reserved for funerals, his freshly polished sheriff's badge gleaming from the front pocket. Since it was possible we would be called as witnesses, both Junebug and me had been scrubbed from head to toe and forced to wear our church clothes. Junebug's hair had been plastered down with some kind of new grease his mother had discovered. It did a fair job of keeping the cowlicks in place, but smelled like a combination between axle grease and dried flowers. His wiggling soon had a stain on the side of Uncle Jasper's coat where his head kept bumping into it.

The noise in the theater abruptly subsided as Mr. Proctor and Mrs. Duval entered and made their way to the stage, climbing the makeshift stairs and taking their seats at the table closest to the jury box. They were followed a moment later by the District Attorney, Whit Appleby, who looked decidedly uncomfortable at all of the eyes staring at him while he walked to the front of the auditorium.

Selecting the jury had taken two days, but Judge Bundy had insisted it be done in a back room on an individual basis and not allowed the public to watch. He'd told Scoop it was because the case was so serious, but Uncle Jasper had said it was because he was nearly deaf and wouldn't have been able to hear the juror's answers in the huge theater.

Shortly, a man in a tan jacket walked onto the stage from the side.

"All rise, the 145th Judicial District Court in and for Baldwin County is now in session, the Honorable Judge Lawton Bundy presiding."

The judge walked from the same side of the stage and glanced toward the audience, appearing to miss a step and almost trip as he noted the size of his audience, all of whom were on their feet.

"You may be seated," he said as he sat down.

I turned and looked over my shoulder, managing to catch a glimpse of people not only filling all of the seats but also standing two and three deep in the back. I only saw them for a second before Aunt Sarah grabbed me by the ear and made me turn around.

"Well, I see we have a larger crowd than I'd expected. Before we begin I'd like to make a few things clear. Many of you aren't from around here. While we're always pleased to have guests in Baldwin County, we may do things a little differently here than wherever you're from. Due to the situation with our courthouse

124

we are holding this trial in an unusual setting. Don't let this persuade you that the standard rules for behavior in the courtroom have been relaxed. I see several of you have cameras. Please be advised that the very first time I see a picture being taken I will not only confiscate the camera and film, but will also have the ambitious photographer held in contempt and thrown in jail for thirty days. You can take all the pictures you want outside."

He paused to take a breath and shuffled through the papers in front of him.

"I will not tolerate any disruptive behavior in my courtroom either. Any improper comments or actions will result in immediate expulsion from these proceedings...or worse." He peered at the audience over the top of his glasses.

"Finally, I have decided not to sequester the jury in this case, since a lot of them have families or farms that need tending to. If I find out anyone has approached any of them before this trial is over...well, all I can say is God have mercy on that person because I won't. Now that all of that is out of the way we can get on with things."

"Bailiff, bring in the jury."

The twelve men and women entered in a procession from a side door, where they had apparently been waiting under Cecil's watchful eye. They each sat in the folding wooden chairs placed inside the jury box.

"The court calls the case of the State of Texas versus Julia Duval. What says the State?"

Whit Appleby stood. "The State is ready your honor," he said in a voice that cracked from nervousness.

"What says the Defendant?"

"The Defendant is ready your honor," Mr. Proctor intoned as he half rose from the chair.

"Very well. Mr. Appleby, you may proceed."

The district attorney stood and slowly walked toward the jury box, stopping in front and pausing before he began speaking.

"In our lives there are some people we should be able to trust. First and foremost are our parents, but only slightly behind them are our spouses. That is what makes this crime particularly disturbing folks, the fact that Mr. Ted Duval was murdered by the woman he loved and trusted."

"Under Texas law the prosecution is required to prove the facts alleged here in the indictment." Appleby waved a piece of paper he was holding in his hand.

"We must prove that on or about the 28th day of May, 1974, Julia Duval did intentionally cause the death of Theodore Duval. That's all the law requires us to prove, we're not required to prove her motive or anything else. But I'm here to tell you that during this trial you're going to hear indisputable proof that Mrs. Julia Duval had both motive and opportunity to commit this crime."

"For you see, Ted Duval was killed by a lethal combination. You'll hear testimony from the pathologist who performed an autopsy on his body. The blood work and tissue tests revealed that Mr. Duval had ingested a large quantity of a tranquilizer known as Dalmane. This drug was taken in an amount sufficient to render him unconscious in no more than twenty minutes. After he was unconscious he was placed into Sandy Creek, where he died by drowning."

"I told you the Defendant had the opportunity to murder Mr. Duval, let me explain what I meant. It so happens that Julia Duval has an unlimited prescription for Dalmane. She can get as much, as often, as she wants. But Mr. Proctor will tell you that's no evidence. So what else do we have?"

"Sheriff Jasper Johnson is going to tell you his investigation revealed Mr. Duval had been eating a tuna fish sandwich right before he died. He's also going to tell you the tests that were performed on the sandwich revealed it had been laced with Dalmane. So we know how Mr. Duval ingested the drug."

"And do you know where that sandwich came from? Julia Duval. She bought it at the lunch counter in the drugstore and took it to her husband. But apparently she made a stop first to add her own little ingredient to his lunch. An ingredient that made it easier for her to get what she wanted."

"That brings us to the motive. Why would a woman murder her husband? What possible reason could a renowned poet have for killing her husband, a bestselling author? The answer to this one is simple and probably more disturbing than anything else you'll hear in this trial."

"The simple reason is greed."

"Julia Duval stood to inherit all of her husband's estate if he died. Not only his estate, she also was the beneficiary of a life insurance policy in the amount of $ 250,000.00, and that amount would be doubled if he met his death as a result of other than natural causes."

"So she killed him. She murdered her husband for the money. That's what it all boils down to, she was greedy, wanted the money, and murdered her husband. That's what we'll prove during this trial, and after we're finished there'll be only one possible verdict....guilty."

With those words and a final stare at the jurors, Mr. Appleby turned and walked back to his table.

Percy Proctor remained seated for a few moments, with his chin resting on the tips of his fingers, which were pressed against each other in a position as if he were praying. He rose only after Judge Bundy loudly cleared his throat a few times to get his attention.

He stood and picked up a notepad, glancing at it for a moment, setting it back down before walking over to stand in almost the same spot as where the District Attorney had stood to make his opening statement.

"I'm not going to take up a lot of your time by making a flowery speech, I'd rather let the evidence do my talking for me. But I do need to tell you Mr. Appleby and I agree on a few things," he said. "For one, Mr. Duval is dead."

"For another, he did consume a large quantity of Dalmane and drowned. Other than that, I disagree with him on almost everything."

"This case is based on circumstantial evidence. Mr. Appleby wants you to believe that because Mrs. Duval stood to inherit from her husband then she must have killed him. That's hogwash. Everybody that's married is likely to inherit from their spouse but that sure doesn't mean they're going to kill them. Just having a motive isn't evidence of a crime."

"And as far as opportunity goes, well...we'll cross that bridge when we come to it. I'd just ask you to keep an open mind until you've heard all of the evidence, what's offered by Mr. Appleby and what we show you. By the time we finish with all of that, I think you are indeed going to be able to come to only one conclusion and one verdict. Not guilty."

The show was about to begin.

# CHAPTER 16

"Sheriff, exactly how did you come to be aware there had been a drowning?" Mr. Appleby asked.

"My nephew Joe Ben and his friend Junebug Walker came running into my office and reported it."

"What did you do next?"

So far the trial had been a dud as far as I was concerned. Nobody had broken down and confessed to the crime, nobody had started crying, nothing exciting had happened. Of course, Uncle Jasper was just the first witness and I'd always thought he was pretty tough anyway.

"My deputy, Cecil Parker, and I drove back to Sandy Creek with the boys. They showed us where they'd been when they saw the body and I went downstream from there until I came to a point in the creek where a bunch of logs and other debris had piled up. As I suspected, that's where the body turned out to be caught."

"You've referred to 'the body' several times. Did you subsequently learn the identity of the decedent?"

"Yes we did. It was Theodore Duval."

"What did you do after you found the corpse?"

"We pulled it out of the water and waited for the ambulance to arrive. They took the body away and we came back to town."

"Did you return to the crime scene later?"

"Yes. Later that day I drove back out to the woods near the creek to see if I could find anything that might help me determine what had happened."

"And what did you find?"

"In a small clearing not far from the creek there was a folding lawn chair with a writing tablet on it. On the ground next to the chair was a half eaten tuna fish sandwich and a soda can that had been knocked over. There also appeared to be a trail leading down to the creek."

"Do you have an opinion as to how Mr. Duval ended up in the creek?"

"I do."

"What is that opinion?"

"I believe Mr. Duval was rendered unconscious by the Dalmane and then carried or dragged to the creek and dumped in."

"How can you be sure he didn't walk to the creek and fall in?"

"Someone had taken the time to carefully brush the trail with a branch and wipe away all of the footprints. To me it appeared more like someone was trying to destroy evidence rather than someone who accidentally fell into a creek."

"How did you determine a branch was used to sweep the trail?"

"Well, I could tell the trail had been swept so I checked the creek and sure enough, I found a branch down a ways that had been freshly cut. I can't say for sure it was the one that was used, but I can say for sure the trail was swept with something."

"What did you do next?"

"We took pictures of the area around the chair and the creek. Then we returned to town to continue our investigation."

"Did you turn up any new evidence?"

"Yes. I had received information that Mr. Duval had been staying at Bessie's...I mean Mrs. Hardeman's boarding house. I went there to check things out."

"What did you find?"

"Mr. Duval's room had been ransacked by someone. We weren't able to determine if anything was missing, although it's possible all or a portion of a manuscript he'd been working on had been taken."

"Did you find anything relevant to this case in your search of the room?"

"Yes, in a later search I found a copy of Mr. Duval's will in which he left all of his estate to Julia Duval."

"Did you ever speak with Mrs. Duval prior to her arrest?"

"Yes, on more than one occasion."

"What did she say?"

"She was actually the one who revealed she had gotten Mr. Duval's tuna fish sandwich for him. She also told me she and her husband had been separated for a while and the subject of divorce was mentioned briefly."

"At what point did Julia Duval become a suspect?"

"Probably when I determined she was his sole heir. This gave her the motive, although I wanted to do some more investigation before I made any kind of accusation."

"Could you summarize for the jury why you believe Mrs. Duval committed this murder?"

"Sure. Mr. Duval was drugged through the use of a medication for which Mrs. Duval had a prescription. She was apparently the last person, other than the deceased, to have contact with the sandwich containing the drug. Then there was the fact that she was familiar with his habits and knew he preferred to write in a remote location. When you add this to the fact that she stood to inherit not only his estate but also a sizeable insurance policy it all added up."

"Could you tell us a little bit about the insurance policy?"

"It had a face value of $ 250,000.00 but in the event of a death by other than natural causes it paid double, or $500,000,00."

"And who was the beneficiary of this policy?"

"Julia Duval."

I saw several of the jurors looking at Mrs. Duval with a hard look in their eyes.

Mr. Appleby continued questioning Uncle Jasper, filling in the details of the investigation and clearing up hazy areas of testimony. Eventually I saw one of the jurors yawn. Appleby apparently saw as well and abruptly cut his questioning off.

Mr. Proctor looked at his notes.

"Sheriff, you're not trying to tell this jury anyone saw Mrs. Duval commit any type of crime are you?

"No sir. There were no eyewitnesses as far as I know."

"Was there anyone that told you the Dalmane in the sandwich was out of the bottle prescribed for Mrs. Duval?"

"No."

"In fact there's no way you can tell where it came from is there?"

"No."

"So that we're clear for the jury, Mr. Duval's chair in the woods was overturned?"

"Yes."

"Did the site suggest he'd been seated in the chair when the drug took effect?"

"That's my belief. I think he may have tried to get up but was unable to. He then fell out of the chair, causing it to overturn, and probably lay there by the chair until he was dragged to the creek and thrown in."

"Are you a pretty good judge of size Sheriff?"

"What do you mean?"

"Well, how tall would you say Julia Duval is?" Mr. Proctor pulled her chair back and she stood up.

Uncle Jasper looked at her for a moment.

"I'd say about 5'3"."

"Very good Sheriff, I believe that's exactly right. How much do you think she weighs?"

"In the neighborhood of 120 pounds."

132

"Again, very astute. Did you have a chance to look at Mr. Duval?"

"Yes I did."

"And what size was he?"

"He was a fairly large man. I'd say probably six feet tall and weighing, I'd guess, about two hundred and twenty five pounds."

"And it's your belief that Julia Duval, this petite young thing, dragged a man who was nearly double her size all the way from the camp site to the creek, then dumped him in?"

"Well....yes, that's the way I believe it happened."

"You would agree with me that would be a chore for someone of her size?"

"Yes, she would have had to struggle I'm sure."

"A few final questions Sheriff. It is important in an investigation to get as much information as you can isn't it?"

"Yes. I'd agree with that."

"And if you're relying on information supplied by someone else, then find out the information they supplied you was missing some very large facts, that would cast some suspicion on their observations wouldn't it?"

"I imagine I'd take their opinion with a grain of salt."

"Thank you Sheriff. I have no more questions."

"You may step down Sheriff. The State may call their next witness."

"The State calls Dr. Donald Everett."

A distinguished looking man with gray hair and wire rimmed spectacles walked up the aisle and onto the stage, then took his place on the witness stand after being sworn in.

"Would you state your name and occupation for the jury?"

"Yes sir. My name is Donald Everett. I'm a coroner."

"Can you explain exactly what a coroner is?"

"Actually I'm a medical doctor but rather than diagnosing patients I examine and test bodies to determine the cause of death. As far as education I go through the same programs as someone that has a medical practice. In fact, I was in private practice for fifteen years before I accepted the offer to become the coroner."

"How long have you been practicing as coroner?"

"Just over ten years."

"Is it a part of your job to perform autopsies?"

"Yes it is."

"In your ten years how many would you say you've performed?"

"I do between four and ten a week. I calculated it last year and figured I've done at least twenty five hundred autopsies."

"Have these been on people that died from a variety of causes?"

"Yes. Many died in automobile collisions, some were shot, others stabbed, some poisoned, some beaten...I've seen almost every way a person can die or be killed."

"Did you have occasion to work on a case involving a body later identified as Ted Duval?"

"Yes I did. The body was transported to me on the day it was found."

"Did you perform an examination?"

"Yes."

"What did you find?"

"I made an initial determination from the corpse's outward appearance that the body had been submerged in water for an extended period of time. I suspected the cause of death would be drowning or drowning related."

134

"What did you do next?"

"I performed an autopsy."

"What is that?"

"Basically you cut into the corpse and take samples of blood and tissues and the contents of the stomach, lungs, that kind of thing. What you're really doing is performing an internal examination to determine the cause of death."

"Were you able to make a determination?"

"Yes. It was apparent from the quantity of water and other materials in the corpse's lungs and stomach that he had drowned. If he had been placed in the water after death we would have found some of these in the stomach and lungs but not to this degree."

"Could you explain that a little further?"

"Sure. Let's say that someone is shot, and the body is then dumped into a lake. Some amount of the lake water and sediment will work its way into the lungs and stomach, just because the water naturally tries to fill in all spaces. In the case of a drowning victim there is a greater volume because they are physically and actively replacing the empty spaces in their stomach and lungs with the water."

"Is that what you found in this case?"

"Yes."

"Did your tests reveal anything else?"

"Yes. The blood and tissue tests showed that Mr. Duval was heavily under the influence of a drug called Flurazapam, commonly known and prescribed under the brand name Dalmane. This was not only present in the blood and tissues, but also detectable in the stomach contents."

"What exactly is Dalmane?"

"It is a tranquilizer quite often prescribed and used as a sleeping pill."

"What effect would this have had on Mr. Duval?"

"As the drug took effect it would have slowed his respiratory system down considerably. The lack of oxygen caused by the decreased breathing would have made him grow lethargic and sleepy. Eventually he would have been unable to remain awake."

"You mentioned the stomach contents showed Dalmane was present in the stomach. Why is this significant?"

"Initially it was significant because it demonstrated the most likely method the drug was ingested, orally as opposed to being injected for instance. Later this would prove important because Sheriff Johnson was able to provide what we believe was the source of the drug."

"What was that exactly?"

"As Sheriff Johnson testified earlier, he found a partially consumed tuna fish sandwich in close proximity to where the victim was apparently located when the drug took effect. He sent this sandwich to me for testing. Those tests revealed an extremely high concentration of the drug within the sandwich."

"So in your opinion what was the cause of Mr. Duval's death?"

"In my opinion he ingested a large quantity of a tranquilizer which rendered him unconscious. At some point shortly after that he was placed into a creek and subsequently drowned. So I guess it was really a combination of a drug overdose and drowning, but the drowning is actually what killed him."

Just then Junebug started whispering furiously to Uncle Jasper, who appeared to argue with him for a moment, then scooted back in his seat and let Junebug edge past and run up the aisle toward the rear of the theater.

A few minutes later he reappeared. As the door opened I heard a familiar noise coming from the back of the auditorium. My friend strolled to the end of our aisle. Cradled in his arms was a large box of popcorn,

136

sparking the realization that what I had heard was the sound of kernels popping. The odor of popcorn wafted through the theater.

"What are you doing?" Uncle Jasper whispered furiously to Junebug.

"I was hungry."

"I thought you were going to the bathroom."

"I did. I just made a detour on the way back."

I suddenly realized the testimony from the stage had stopped.

"Young man, what is that in your arms?"

Junebug's eyes got real wide as he realized the judge was talking to him.

"Sir?"

"I asked you what you were carrying?"

"Popcorn, your majesty."

Guffaws of laughter could be heard from around the room."

Judge Bunton unsuccessfully tried to hide a smile behind his hand.

"Young fellow, the proper term for a judge is 'Your Honor', not 'Your Majesty'. Now aside from that, where did you get that popcorn?"

"At the snack bar, your maj...I mean, your honor."

The judge leaned down and whispered to the bailiff, who walked off of the stage and disappeared through the back door. Gradually, the popping sound faded.

"Ladies and gentleman, this is a court of law even though we are forced to convene in an unusual place. Eating and drinking in this court will not be tolerated."

Junebug was standing in the aisle, looking unsure as to what he should do.

"However, I am going to make a special exception for the young man who has already made his

137

purchase." He looked down at Junebug. "You may eat your popcorn, but please try to be as quiet as possible."

Mr. Appleby resumed his questioning as Junebug wormed his way into his seat.

After a few minutes I reached across in front of Aunt Sarah and snagged a handful of the popcorn.

Junebug leaned forward and hissed, "Do you want to get us both in trouble? The judge said nobody else could eat but me."

I finished my portion and was trying to plan my attack so I could snag another fistful when Junebug suddenly began hacking and coughing.

Mr. Appleby turned to look at us, his expression showing his displeasure at the interruption.

Junebug continued gagging and coughing, indifferent to the effect he was having on the proceedings.

"What's wrong with him?" Judge Bunton asked.

Uncle Jasper was pounding him on the back to no avail.

"I think he's got a piece of popcorn caught in his throat," I offered.

"Well somebody get him something to drink so we can start this trial again."

A man came running down the aisle carrying a bottle of RC Cola and handed it to Junebug, who gratefully took a sip and immediately quieted down.

The questioning resumed and I leaned forward and whispered to Junebug, "Are you all right?"

He glanced up to be sure Aunt Sarah had her attention focused on the proceedings.

"I wasn't really choking, just thirsty. Want a sip?" He offered the bottle and I gratefully took a swig. As I handed it back he held his package of popcorn out for me to share.

I turned my attention back to the stage just as Mr. Appleby finished his questioning and Mr. Proctor started.

"Dr. Everett, would you agree with me that there was no way to tell from Mr. Duval's body who was responsible for his death?" he asked.

"Yes, I'd agree with that."

"Would you also agree that the more information you provide, the more effective an investigation would be?"

"Generally speaking, yes I'd agree with that."

"Did you do a thorough autopsy on Mr. Duval's body?"

"Yes, I think so."

"Did you find anything else unusual during the autopsy?"

He looked puzzled. "No, not that I can recall."

"Would you agree with me that if indeed something was missed in the autopsy, it would reflect negatively on the accuracy of the other information obtained?"

"I guess it could."

Mr. Proctor stood. "No more questions your honor."

# CHAPTER 17

Mr. Appleby called a few more witnesses to testify, including the druggist from Tyler who had filled Mrs. Duval's prescription a few days before Mr. Duval disappeared and then again two weeks later. The only questions Mr. Proctor asked were about the reason given for the refill by his client, which the pharmacist said she explained to him was because she had dropped the other bottle into the toilet when her makeup case fell.

By this time the jurors were all giving her hard looks, obviously leaning toward a guilty verdict. I was surprised by the lack of effort on Mr. Proctor's part, since he rarely asked more than a few questions in his cross examination.

After the state rested its case, Percy Proctor stood up and made a half hearted motion to dismiss the case, which the judge quickly denied.

"Mr. Proctor, you may call your first witness."

"We would call George Wharton to the stand."

A small man carrying a scuffed briefcase made his way to the stage.

"Please state your name for the jury."

"George Wharton."

"Mr. Wharton, what is your occupation?"

"I am an accountant with the firm of Landry, Oldham and Lott, in Houston, Texas."

"I understand you are in a little bit of a hurry today."

"Yes sir. I am in the middle of a rather extensive audit of an investment firm that is handling a portion of one of my client's funds."

"Who is that client?"

"Julia Duval."

"Does Mrs. Duval do quite a bit of business with your firm?"

"Yes, she is one of our better clients."

"There was some testimony earlier today concerning her inheriting slightly more than half a million dollars on Mr. Duval's death. Will this significantly increase her net worth?"

"Well, half a million dollars is a significant sum, but in the scheme of things it will represent a very, very small portion of her total worth."

"Could you please explain to the jury exactly why this is?"

"Certainly." The small man turned to face the jury panel. "Julia Duval is the only child of Jackson Gates, who owned the 150,000 acre Gates Ranch in West Texas. In addition to the oil royalties the family accumulated he was also a shrewd investor who parlayed his earnings into a fortune worth many times its original amount."

"Exactly what is Julia Duval's net worth?"

"I'm not sure precisely, I don't have all of her portfolio with me, but I do know that in addition to the ranch and oil royalties she earns more than a half a million dollars a year in interest alone. She never spends anywhere near all of it so the amounts just keep growing"

"So the chance of gaining a half a million dollars wouldn't be as large a temptation to her as it would to a lot of people?"

"Absolutely not. Let me also add I've known Julia Duval since she was a child, and have never seen her harm or even raise her voice to anyone. That young woman could not commit a murder."

"I believe we'll pass the witness."

Mr. Appleby raised his head off of his hands and asked a few half-hearted questions, but was obviously unprepared for this witness and a major blow to his case in the loss of a motive. Within ten minutes Mr. Wharton was dismissed and on his way back to Houston.

"Next witness," Judge Bunton said.

"The defense would call Dr. Lawrence Hester."

I'd never heard his name and looked at Uncle Jasper, who just shrugged to indicate he didn't recognize the doctor's name either.

After a few minutes of introduction and discussion of the doctor's education Mr. Proctor went to the meat of the matter.

"Dr. Hester, you've been present throughout the testimony in this case haven't you?"

"Yes I have."

"Have you heard anything that you disagree with?"

"Yes. First, the sheriff testified Mr. Duval was dragged quite a distance from a location in the woods and then dumped in the creek."

"Do you disagree that was what happened?"

"Oh no, I didn't mean to say that. If the sheriff's investigation indicated the victim was dragged to the creek I am sure that's how it occurred."

"Then what did you mean?"

"I mean this is a clear indication Mrs. Duval could not have committed this crime."

"Why do you say that?"

"I've been Julia and Ted Duval's personal physician for a number of years. From outward appearances Julia Duval is perfectly healthy and in fine physical shape, but in reality she suffers from heart problems."

"What do you mean?"

"Simply put, Mrs. Duval is limited in the amount of physical exertion she can stand. I can say that without a doubt if Julia Duval had tried to drag a man of Ted Duval's build even ten yards there would have been at least one more body out there. Her heart couldn't have taken the strain."

"Are you sure of this?"

"As sure as it is possible to be of any medical diagnosis."

"So to sum it up what would your opinion be as to whether or not Julia Duval could have committed the acts the sheriff was talking about?"

"I believe it was physically impossible without causing her to have a heart attack."

Mr. Proctor paused and looked at the jury box where several of the jurors were now looking on with interest.

"Was there anything else you heard that surprised you?"

"As a matter of fact, yes. I am aware of Dr. Everett's reputation as a fine coroner so I was a little surprised he missed something so obvious."

"What was that?"

"Ted Duval had a brain tumor which should have been obvious during a complete autopsy. It had grown to slightly larger than a peanut."

"What was his prognosis?"

"It was inoperable. Ted Duval would have been dead in about a year even if this hadn't happened."

"Do you have any explanation as to why this would have been missed by Dr. Everett?"

"On your request I reviewed his autopsy notes and it appears he made a finding that Mr. Duval was killed by the lethal combination of being under the influence of Dalmane when he entered the creek. Once this determination was made he apparently stopped looking any further."

"Do you know if anything else of significance was missed? If there were any clues which remain undiscovered?"

"No, there is no way to tell. The only reason I know he missed the brain tumor was that I made the original diagnosis. From an incomplete autopsy you can only tell what was found, not what was there and missed. If I hadn't been personally acquainted with Mr. Duval I would have never know he had a brain tumor from what the autopsy showed."

Mr. Appleby attempted to repair what damage he could by recalling Dr. Everett, but probably only made things worse. When questioned Dr. Everett admitted he stopped looking once the cause of death was determined. His assertion to the jury that it was extremely unlikely any other evidence existed appeared to fall on deaf ears.

The jury was out only twenty five minutes before returning a verdict of not guilty.

# CHAPTER 18

The theater erupted as the reporters exploded from their seats and ran out the exits, I assumed to be the first to call in their stories at the few available public telephones in town. Uncle Jasper stood and edged past Aunt Sarah into the aisle, then walked toward the stage and up the stairs. I hesitated a moment, then hurried to catch up with him, Junebug following on my heels.

Percy Proctor had just finished accepting a hug from Julia Duval, who watched Uncle Jasper approach. She winked at me and I smiled and winked back.

"Percy, I need to talk to you in private for a minute."

"Certainly. Mrs. Duval if you wouldn't mind waiting over there," he motioned toward the side door where Cecil was standing. She walked over and stood next to the deputy, who looked uncomfortable and unsure of what to do.

"Cecil," Uncle Jasper said, "you make sure nobody bothers her while we're talking."

Cecil nodded.

Uncle Jasper took Mr. Proctor by the arm and pulled him a little further toward the now empty table the District Attorney had hastily withdrawn from following the verdict.

"Percy, you know I've always thought you played fast and loose with the rules but I think you're basically honest and I have to have a question answered."

Mr. Proctor glanced at Junebug and me then looked back at Uncle Jasper and raised an eyebrow questioningly.

"It's okay. They can listen."

"All right then, what's your question?"

"Did she do it?"

"Jasper, you know I can't answer that."

"Listen to me, this isn't a game. If she did it then I can shut the case and quit looking for the killer, since she can't be tried again for Ted Duval's murder. But if she didn't kill him that means there's still a murderer loose out there and I need to get busy."

Percy Proctor just looked at Uncle Jasper for a minute, then shook his head.

"As much as I'd like to, I just can't answer your question. If anybody ever found out I'd be disbarred."

Uncle Jasper's ears started turning red.

"I should have known better than to ask. Especially after the things you've done before."

Mr. Proctor turned and walked back to his table, where he was met by Mrs. Duval. He leaned over and whispered to her and she whispered something back.

Uncle Jasper had already walked down the stair and started up the aisle when Mr. Proctor spoke.

"Jasper."

He stopped and looked back.

"Don't close your case, you've still got work to do."

My uncle stood and stared at the lawyer for a moment.

"Thanks. I appreciate it."

Mr. Proctor waved his hand at him, implying it was no big deal.

Uncle Jasper had taken only a few more steps when he was stopped again.

"Jasper."

Once more he turned toward the lawyer on the stage, who was looking down at the papers he was putting into his briefcase.

"Do you remember that moonshine case? The one where the liquid in the bottles turned out to be

146

water?"

"Yes."

"You always thought I switched bottles on you somehow didn't you?"

"Yes. I tasted it myself when we seized it. That was liquor in those bottles."

"I don't doubt you a bit, I'm sure it was liquor, but I didn't switch bottles or tamper with the evidence in any way."

"No? Then how do you explain the water being in there?"

Mr. Proctor chuckled to himself for a minute while we stood there and waited.

"You know, I heard a story one time. It seems there was this police officer in charge of storing the evidence over in Sumter. This officer had a bad drinking problem, both on duty and off. The problem was even worse because he had control over the largest supply of liquor in Baldwin County, the seized booze stored in the evidence room. It also seems he was aware people might notice a bottle being half empty, so anytime he took a nip from a bottle under his care, he was always careful to replace whatever he drank with tap water. It also seems this lawyer knew his habit and knew the officer put a little pencil mark on the bottles so he would be able to tell at what level the liquid was supposed to be. So this lawyer kept putting the case off and putting the case off until he figured the bottles had mostly water in them. And as it turned out he was right. But at no time did this lawyer ever do anything to any of those bottles or the liquid inside of them, he just took advantage of a little bit of information he had that nobody else did. Does that clear things up?"

"It certainly does, Percy. It also seems like there was this sheriff who didn't like losing and who just assumed if he did lose, it was because the other side was cheating. It appears this sheriff has been wrong on several counts."

"Like I've said before, Jasper, it's all a game. We can't afford the luxury of looking at things as black and white. It's all just shades of gray. Sometimes you need to forget all your preconceived notions and examine everything with an open mind, just start from scratch."

"I'll bear that in mind. Thanks again."

"No problem, Sheriff." He latched his briefcase. "Now if you would be so kind as to have your deputy escort us out, I think Mrs. Duval and I would like to avoid having to give any interviews right now."

"Cecil, you help these two to their cars."

"Thanks," Mr. Proctor said. "Now I guess I need to go see my next falsely accused client. I'm in such a generous mood I may even just let the prosecutor just dismiss the charges without having to make an apology. Or at least not a public one." With that he placed the straw hat on top of his head and left the scene of his victory.

\*\*\*\*\*\*\*\*\*\*\*\*\*\*\*\*\*\*\*\*\*\*\*\*

"You boys head on home. I need some time to think things through," Uncle Jasper said after we'd made our way through the throng of reporters and onlookers waiting outside the Bijou.

"Aw Sheriff. I bet we could be a lot of help," Junebug pled.

"No, not this time. I'll come by and get you if I come up with anything important, but y'all make too much noise to be around right now."

I could tell by the look on his face there wasn't any use in arguing and so we separated at the next corner, Uncle Jasper heading to his office and me and Junebug wandering in the general direction of my house.

"Do you want to go fishing?" I asked after we'd walked a few blocks in silence.

"Naw, better not. We probably need to stay close by in case something happens."

"How about a game of Monopoly?"

"Too boring. I'm in the mood for something exciting."

Just then a car pulled up next to us.

"Hey fellows, do you know where I can find the...," the man peering out the passenger window stopped talking all of a sudden. "Say aren't you two the boys that found the body and are trying to solve that old bank robbery now?"

"Sure are," Junebug replied.

The engine shut off and the passengers and driver's doors opened, with a man stepping out of each. They appeared to be in their early fifties

"We're sure glad to meet you. As a matter of fact, I was just about to ask where you lived."

"What for?" Junebug asked.

"Where are my manners? My name is Larry Freeman and this is my associate, Matt Gilmore. We're reporters with a television station in Charleston, South Carolina."

"Nice to meet you," Junebug and I said at the same time.

"Nice to meet you boys. We were hoping to get a chance to talk to you concerning the story about y'all investigating that bank robbery from back in the fifties."

"Sure, we'll be glad to talk to you. What do you want to know?" Junebug asked.

"I hate to talk out here in this heat. How about if we buy you fellows an ice cream? It'd be a lot more comfortable talking somewhere that was air conditioned."

I spoke up. "That'd be all right. How about if we meet you over at the drug store?"

"Oh there's no need for y'all to walk all that way. Why don't you ride with us?" Mr. Freeman said as the other man opened the door and folded his seat forward so we could climb into the back seat.

"We appreciate the offer, but we're not allowed to ride with people we don't know," I said.

"But you do know us. We just introduced ourselves." Mr. Freeman smiled and for a moment I wavered since he looked so friendly, then remembered how serious Uncle Jasper had been when he'd warned about what would happen if he ever caught me breaking this particular rule.

"I'm sorry. I don't want to be rude, but my uncle said there weren't any exceptions."

"That's an excellent rule, but you know what?"

"What?" Junebug asked suspiciously.

"I'm afraid I'm going to have to insist."

I started backing up, and glanced down as my heel caught on a crack in the sidewalk. When I looked back up Mr. Gilmore had the corner of his jacket pulled back just enough to reveal the handle of a pistol sticking out of the waistband of his pants.

"As he said boys, we insist. Now get in the car." He must have seen something in my eyes because he added, "And don't make any noise or attract any attention because if you do I promise you'll regret it more than we will."

# CHAPTER 19

Junebug and I looked at each other, but didn't appear to have any choice in the matter. I swallowed hard and climbed into the back seat, followed by my friend. He took his hat off as he sat back and just before our captor closed the door, dropped it on the ground.

The car pulled away from the curb and proceeded down the street.

"You two lay on the floorboard and be quiet. If I see either one of you raise up or hear you make a sound...well, I'd just better not."

We hunkered down, each with our feet against a side of the car and with our heads close together.

"What do we do now?" he whispered to me.

"Shoot, I don't know. What would the Hardy Boys do?"

"They'd plan some kind of brilliant escape but I can't think of anything."

"Me neither."

I recognized a billboard as it flashed by the window on the other side.

"They're taking us out Highway 6."

We laid there in silence for a few minutes although I could almost hear the wheels turning in Junebug's head.

The car slowed down and I heard the turn signal begin clicking.

"I'm gonna be sick," Junebug suddenly wailed.

"Quit griping. You're okay," the man in the passenger seat said. I noticed a big hairy mole on the back of his neck.

"I'm not kidding, I'm about to puke up all of that chicken gumbo and turnip greens I had for lunch."

He reached over and plucked my lucky bandanna out of my pocket where I always carried it wadded up. Uncle Jasper had once taken me to a Dallas Cowboys game and Roger Staubach had wiped his face with this very bandanna, then thrown it to me as he walked off the field. I figured anything that Roger Staubach had touched must be lucky. Aunt Sarah had been on me to throw it away since the time Jake had nearly swallowed it, being prevented only by me and Junebug chasing him down, grabbing the inch or so still visible and then pulling the sodden cloth from down his throat.

"Damn," the driver said and pulled the car over. He jumped out and looked down the road both ways.

"All right, you can get out. But if you try anything funny..."

"I know, I know, I'll be sorry," Junebug said as he climbed out past the passenger.

I started to raise up and look around but stopped when the man still in the front seat said, "You just stay put. I'm not going to take a chance with both of you loose out here."

After a while I heard Junebug's voice from outside the car.

"Must have just been the heat and gasoline fumes. If y'all will leave the windows down that'd probably help."

"How do I know you won't start hollering?"

"Mister, who's got the gun? Besides, who'd hear me out here?"

The man just grunted as Junebug reentered the car and once again lay on the floorboard. Within a couple of seconds we were moving.

"What was that about?" I asked him when he'd settled in and the noise from the road would help cover our voices.

"I wanted to see where we were."

"Where are we?"

152

"We'd just turned onto Johnson Branch road."

"Did anybody see you?"

"Nope. Not a car in sight."

I was quiet for a moment.

"You didn't puke on my lucky rag did you?"

"Not exactly."

"What do you mean 'not exactly'?"

"Well, not a full puke anyway. Just a small splash."

"If you just wanted to look around why'd you throw up?"

"Had to make it look real. Let me tell you something, gumbo and greens are not a good choice for lunch when you might have to barf later."

"If you don't shut up I'll know for myself," I said. "Can I have my bandanna back?"

"No."

"Why not?"

"I used it to mark our trail."

"What are you boys jabbering about?" A voice from the front seat asked.

"I told him I was still feeling a little sick. Could you roll the back windows down?"

I heard the sound of the electric motors whirring and saw the window behind Junebug lower.

"Thanks," he said.

"What do we do now?" I whispered.

"I'm going to try and throw things out every now and then so that somebody can find us."

"Be careful they don't see you."

Every little while I'd see him flick something out the window.

"What are you throwing?"

"Everything in my pockets. String, change, everything I've got, plus a paycheck stub and a handful of paper napkins I found on the floorboard. What do you have?"

"Nothing else. All I had was my bandanna."

153

He looked exasperated. "You sure aren't prepared."

"Junebug, I really didn't have any reason to suspect we'd be in this situation."

"Always be prepared, that's my motto."

I didn't answer. I'd always assumed his motto was "do unto others before they do unto you."

After a while the car stopped and the two men got out, leaning the seats forward and motioning us to exit.

The car was parked in front of a shack underneath some pine trees. We had obviously turned off of the main dirt road since the only visible way in was a logging road leading back into the trees.

Just behind and to one side of the shack was a wire pen containing one of the biggest, meanest looking dogs I'd ever seen. He looked like the result of a wolf being cross bred with a wolverine, with an added dose of chain saw for good measure. His frenzied attempts to claw his way through the cage combined with the ferocious snarling and saliva spraying from his curled back lips indicated his preferred meal of choice was strangers, preferably tender young twelve year old strangers.

"This is it boys, our home sweet home...at least for a while. You're miles from anywhere and if you try to escape we'll catch you before you make it back to town. Old Hammer there," he motioned toward the dog, "will make sure of that." He wandered over and opened the door to the shack. "You boys come on in. We need to get better acquainted."

\*\*\*\*\*\*\*\*\*\*\*\*\*\*\*\*\*\*\*\*\*\*\*

We'd been sitting tied in the chairs for the better part of two hours.

"You boys are going to have to tell us at some point."

"We told you already, we don't know anything,"

154

I said again.

The men were apparently convinced that Junebug and I had really figured out who the robbers were. By this time I knew a safe bet would be that these two had been involved, but still didn't know who they were.

"Mister, if we knew anything we'd tell you so fast it'd make your head swim so you'd untie us and let us go." My heart dropped as he said this last part because the two men glanced at one another, then quickly looked back at us. I'd just gotten the distinct feeling they weren't just going to untie us and let us go on our merry way.

"Come on. You told the reporter you almost had the crime solved. We just want to know what you know."

"Why are you so curious?"

I kicked Junebug under the table.

"We don't care why you're curious. Just believe me when I tell you we don't know anything about the robbery that everybody else doesn't know. Junebug was just running his mouth and has got us into trouble," I pointedly looked at my friend, "again. He was just bragging."

"I sure wish we could believe you, but we were told to keep you here until we were sure you had told us everything and I'm just not convinced you have. Why would anybody lie to a big newspaper about something like that?"

"Mister, you'd just have to know Junebug. If you did you'd understand."

From the look my pal was giving me I knew he wasn't particularly happy about my comments, but figured he'd forgive and forget if we got out of this okay.

"Maybe if you have a while to think about it you'll change your minds and talk to us. Matt, why don't you escort these two to the back room?"

We were yanked out of the chairs by our ropes and semi-dragged into the back room by the man with the mole. He dumped us on the floor then slammed the door shut, locking it from the outside with a distinctive "click".

"So, what now?" I whispered as soon as I heard the footsteps move away from the door.

"Now we wait and think."

I must have nodded off in the heat as we lay there because I suddenly noticed the light coming through the cracks in the wall and from under the door was a lot dimmer.

"Joe Ben, wake up."

"I'm awake."

"Let's try to get out of these ropes. My nose itches and I'm fixing to explode if I don't scratch it."

I heard Junebug start wiggling, but it was too dim in there to see what he was doing. At least not until he kicked me dead square in the middle of the face with his sneakers.

After the stars and lights quit exploding I hissed at him, "Darn it Junebug, quit before you kill me."

He stopped moving.

"Sorry."

I tasted a warm, coppery liquid begin trickling down my lip.

"Now see what you've gone and done. You've got my nose to bleeding."

"I said I was sorry."

"I was better off with the kidnappers. At least they didn't try to break my nose."

"Quit being a sissy. It was an accident."

"That doesn't make it hurt any less."

He wiggled around until his face was right up close to mine and peered at my nose.

"Yup, it's bleeding all right. Bleeding like a stuck hog. I don't remember when I've ever seen it bleed like that. Even the time you let me try to knock

156

that apple off your head with a baseball didn't make it gush like this. I sure hope it don't make you sick because..."

"Junebug would you shut up. The only thing making me sick is the smell of your breath. Back up."

He wiggled a little further back.

"You didn't have to try and hurt my feelings."

"You try having somebody that smells like puked up gumbo and turnip greens breathing on you while you've got a mouthful of blood and see how you like it."

He didn't say anything for a while, just laid there wiggling his arms, trying to loosen the ropes holding his hands tied behind his back.

"Say Joe Ben, why don't you let me borrow a little of that blood."

"What? Junebug Walker have you lost your mind? What in the world do you want blood for?"

Normally I'd have been afraid to ask that question, but since he was tied up I didn't see where there was much he could do to make our situation worse.

"I want you to worm your way toward my arms and I'll try to move them toward you so that we can see if the blood will make my wrists slick enough to slide the ropes off."

I didn't see how it could hurt anything.

"Okay."

I'd nearly made it to his wrists when his elbow caught me square in the nose, making those stars and lights explode again.

"Darn it Junebug, did they pay you to kill me or something?"

"It'd almost stopped bleeding."

"That's what it's supposed to do."

"Yeah, but not till we see if it'll loosen the ropes."

"You mean you did it on purpose?"

157

"Sure. You don't think I'm clumsy enough to accidentally do it twice do you?"

"Why didn't you warn me?"

"I figured it'd hurt less if you weren't expecting it. Plus you might have said no."

"Of course I'd have said no, have you lost your mind?"

"That's why I didn't tell you. It was easier to get in a good shot without you trying to dodge out of the way."

To Junebug I guess he made good sense, but I silently promised myself I owed him a payback if we ever got out of this mess...and if I didn't bleed to death first.

"Well hurry up and try to get loose," I said, then added emphatically, "and don't hit me again or I'll bite you so hard they'll have to pry my teeth off of you with a crowbar."

He shifted a bit and I raised my head up off of the floor so the blood and snot would drip down onto his skinny wrists. We stayed like that until the flow from my nostrils began slacking off.

"If you don't mind I'll lay down now and try to get the bleeding to stop. It seems to me like I read somewhere you've got to have at least a little bit of blood left for your heart to work right."

"Sissy," he mumbled.

I heard that monster they'd called Hammer begin his frenzied barking, followed a moment later by the sound of a car door slamming out front. The floorboards creaked as somebody walked across the front porch and opened the door. This was followed shortly by muffled voices from the next room.

"Can you hear what they're saying?" I asked Junebug, who was still trying to get loose.

"Naw...dang it. I almost had 'em loose."

At that moment I heard the key unlocking the door.

"Quit Junebug, they're fixing to come in."

The light from the other room, while dimmer than it had been when we'd been in there earlier, was still bright enough to make us squint. One of the men raised my head up with his hand and tied some kind of rag around my eyes, blindfolding me. I heard a commotion next to me and assumed the other was doing the same to Junebug.

"What have you got all over you?" the man handling me asked.

I didn't respond, so he just grunted and carried me into the other room. I heard a thump followed immediately by Junebug's exclamation "Ouch!" as he was apparently dropped next to me.

"What happened to them?" a new voice, obviously one the owner was attempting to disguise, asked.

"I don't know. They were fine when we put them in there," the voice belonging to the man called Matt Gilmore replied.

"Didn't I tell you not to hurt them yet?"

I didn't like that word 'yet' at all.

"We didn't. I told you they were fine when we put them in there."

"It's just a bloody nose," I said.

"Are you two ready to talk yet?" Now the one who had identified himself as Larry Freeman in the beginning spoke up.

"We've been ready to talk the whole time. You two just wouldn't listen," Junebug said.

"I mean are you ready to talk about the robbery?"

"We've already told you everything we know. Do you want us to start making things up just to keep you occupied?"

"Junebug, hush," I said, then spoke to the new voice. "I don't know who you are or what you've got to do with this whole thing, but we don't know anything

159

that's not public knowledge. Junebug was just bragging to that reporter. Our investigation has consisted of walking in the bank and looking around and reading all of the old articles, that's it."

"You know, I almost believe you," the new voice said.

"You should because it's the truth."

"But I know Junebug Walker's propensity for prevarication, so maybe we'll just keep you here for a while longer," he said, then added, "You may want to reconsider because you're really of no use to us if you don't know anything."

We were hoisted up and dumped unceremoniously back into the room. As soon as the door was shut and locked, Junebug squirmed over to me.

"Did you recognize the new guy's voice?"

"No, although it did sound familiar."

"There was something about it...but I just can't figure out what."

"He's obviously from around here though."

"What make you say that?"

"Simple, Mr. Detective. Why else would he disguise his voice? Obviously he was afraid we'd recognize it. Plus, he said he knew your propensity for something or other...and face it Junebug, you're not that well known. He has to be from around here."

"That makes sense."

"We'd better figure out what to do though, I've got a feeling that when they finally become convinced we don't know anything they're not just going to send us on our way with a pat on the head and a lollipop for our troubles. They're going to kill us."

# CHAPTER 20

I awoke the next morning stiff and sore all over. Though it had thundered and rained most of the night the storms had apparently passed and sunshine was peeking through the cracks in the wall and coming under the door. My hands were numb from being tied all night and, while normally I didn't mind a little dirt, the combination of dried blood and grime made me feel filthy from head to toe. The rain that had dripped in through the roof hadn't washed off enough filth to matter.

"You all right?" I heard Junebug ask.

"I guess I'll live but I feel worse than I did the day after we tried to come down Mayhaw Hill on our skateboards."

"I know what you mean. At least we won't be picking gravel out of our skin for three weeks though."

"What do you think'll happen today?"

"I don't know, but we need to make our move as soon as we can. Why don't we try to stall them until dark, then make our getaway?"

"How do we do that?"

"I'll think of something. You just go along with whatever I do."

"Okay."

"Hey guys," he yelled. "Guys...I've gotta go to the bathroom." He waited about two seconds, then yelled again. "Guys, I'm not kidding. I've gotta go real bad."

I heard a muted grumbling, then the door opened and the one with the mole, the other one had called him Gilmore, entered.

"Jesus, you boys are a lot of trouble."

"Sorry to be a bother. Maybe you ought to think about this next time you get ready to kidnap somebody."

"You sure got a smart mouth for a kid."

"I hear that a lot."

Freeman laughed from the doorway.

"You know kid, I like you. You remind me of me when I was your age."

"That makes me feel good. Maybe I'll grow up to be a bully too."

The man chuckled and led Junebug away by the collar.

"What about you?" Gilmore asked.

"I could sure use a chance to pee and maybe wash up a little."

They escorted us out on the back porch. An outhouse stood about fifty feet from the back door.

"Would you mind undoing my hands? Unless you want to help me of course?" Junebug asked in a smart aleck tone of voice.

Freeman looked at him for a minute, then motioned to Gilmore.

"All right, cut their hands loose." Then to us he said, "You two don't get any bright ideas unless you want to help us save on food for Hammer."

I glanced over at the pen where the dog was staring at us and licking his chops occasionally.

"Of all the things I could do that would probably be one of my least favorites."

"Smart boy."

Gilmore flicked open a big pocketknife and sliced through the ropes holding my wrists together.

"Thanks," I said as I rubbed my hands together trying to get the circulation going and some feeling back in them.

He just grunted again. I was beginning to think he was the gruntingest, grouchiest person I'd ever met.

Junebug emerged from the bathroom a short while later. As he passed me on my way to the outhouse he winked.

I took a minute to check the inside of the little building for wasp's nests. I'd had a bad experience with wasps in an outhouse some years ago at a family reunion. The resulting episode had left everybody at the party embarrassed except the wasps.

When I was assured I wasn't sharing my private space with anybody I proceeded with my business.

"You two can wash up at hydrant over there." Freeman said when I exited the privy. He pointed to a water pipe coming out of the side of a well pump house, then walked back toward the front of the house and sat on the hood of the car where he could keep an eye on us.

We went over and splashed water on our faces and arms, washing off most of the dried blood. Then we took turns drinking. I hadn't realized how thirsty I was until my first couple of sips. Even though the well water had a sulphur taste, I still thought it was as good as anything I'd ever drank in my life. I took my shirt off and tried to wash some of the dried gore off of it, but had little luck. Junebug was poking around in the little pump house next to me.

"You boys hurry up," Freeman yelled at us without raising from his prone position on the hood.

I saw Junebug stoop down and pick a leaf off the ground.

"Stall him for a minute," he whispered, then stuck his hand back into the pump house.

"Just a minute," I yelled back. "We're trying to wash some of the dried blood and puke off so we don't stink so bad."

"Well, hurry up anyway," the voice yelled back.

"What are you doing?" I whispered to Junebug.

"I'll show you later, let me get there and wash off. You go back and keep 'em busy." He pushed me

163

out of the way and commenced to scrubbing
energetically at his hands. I thought that was unusual
since Junebug had never been one to be overly
concerned about the finer points of hygiene.

"You sure took a long time to not have any
more of a body to clean than you do."

"Sorry."

"Where's your buddy?"

"He's still washing up."

"He's taking too long, I'd better go check on
him."

I thought fast. "I don't think I'd do that."

"Why not?"

"Because that dried puke doesn't smell so good
once it gets wet again. That's what's taking him so
long."

"Maybe I'll just wait a few more minutes. We're
not in any hurry." He lay back down on the hood. I just
stood there next to him, occasionally glancing over at
the dog pen where Hammer stood staring at me and
growling deep in his throat.

Eventually Junebug walked up, soaking wet
from head to toe, but with his hair slicked down and
looking nearly presentable.

"About time. Are y'all hungry?" Freeman asked,
jumping down off of the hood and stretching.

"Starved, we haven't had anything to eat since
lunch yesterday," I said.

Junebug nodded in agreement.

"Let's go inside and get something to eat? Then
we'll sit around and discuss...things."

"Sure," Junebug said. "That'd be great."

"Good, good. That's what I like to do...cooperate
and get along. Makes everybody happy. Now let's eat."

Gilmore wasn't any better a cook than he was
pleasant company. The toast was burnt, the eggs were
cold and greasy, and the bacon wasn't near done. But all
in all, it tasted great. It's amazing how good a spice

164

hunger provides.

After we'd finished eating we went back outside and sat on the porch. Freeman pulled out a knife and started whittling on a stick he'd found while Gilmore fed the scraps to that garbage disposal they called a dog. A breeze was stirring the trees and except for the noises coming from the dog pen and the knowledge that we were prisoners it would have been a fairly peaceful setting.

I glanced up at the sun and could see it was getting close to noon.

"Are you boys about ready to talk?" Freeman asked when he saw me looking around.

"Sure. What do you want to talk about?" Junebug asked.

"Why don't we talk about the bank robbery first, then we'll go from there."

"Okay. We know the bank was robbed in 1952 and that a bank guard and four customers were killed. We know the robbers were never found and they got away with over $ 200,000.00 in cash." Curiously, when I said this the one called Gilmore snorted, then was silenced by a look from Freeman.

"We know the police found the car abandoned outside of St. John, but there were no clues. To this day none of the money has ever shown up and the men have never been caught. It's also the only case my Uncle Jasper has ever been involved in that remained unsolved a year later. That's about all we know."

"You know, it's funny you should mention your Uncle Jasper. I hear he's been asking questions about the bank robbery. Is he opening his investigation again?"

"I don't think he ever closed it. Every year since I've lived with him on the anniversary of the robbery he pulls out his file and goes through it again, looking for clues he may have missed."

"Has he mentioned anything new?"

"No, not to me. I didn't even know he was asking questions about it."

"So that's what this is all about. You think the sheriff is onto something," Junebug said.

"Maybe."

Just then Hammer went berserk, barking and jumping against the fence. The cause of his agitation became clear when we heard a car coming down the road toward the shack.

"Get 'em inside," Freeman said.

Gilmore grabbed us by the arms and pushed us into the main room of the shack. He pulled his pocketknife out and opened it, using it to point at us.

"You two be quiet."

Junebug and I leaned against the front wall, next to where Gilmore stood looking out the window. He appeared to relax when the car came into sight, but didn't move from his vantage point.

Junebug's hand was resting on my arm and I saw him lean his head against the wall and press his eye to a crack. His hand tightened a moment after I heard the car door slam.

"Where are the boys?" I heard.

"They're inside. I sent them in when we heard your car coming.

"Are they blindfolded?"

"I doubt it, I just sent them in."

"Shit," the unknown man exclaimed. "Get them blindfolded before they see me."

"Gilmore!" Freeman yelled. "Tie the rags around their eyes and bring them out."

After the blindfolds were in place we were led back onto the porch.

"Have you fellows decided to cooperate?" The third man asked in his disguised voice.

"We were cooperating, we just don't know anything," Junebug said.

"Why should I believe you?"

"Why should we lie to you? The only way out of this is to tell you what you want to know. We're just kids, what chance do we have of holding out."

"So you're going to stick to your story to the end?"

"Sorry, it's the only story we've got. It's the truth."

"You leave me no choice then. Tie them up."

I felt myself grabbed and pulled to the edge of the porch, where I'd seen a coil of the same scratchy hemp rope they'd used on us earlier. Within moments I was again bound, this time with my feet as well as my hands restrained.

"Take them back inside. You'll need to wait until late tonight to take care of them, we can't take a chance on somebody seeing you two strangers around at the same time two of our local children come up missing."

"I think they're telling the truth. I don't think they know anything," Freeman said.

"Even if they didn't before they do now. They can point the finger at you two...and identify this place."

"So what are we supposed to do with them?"

"What do you think? Kill them and dump the bodies into a creek somewhere."

"Whoa, wait a minute. You never said anything about killing anybody...especially a couple of kids," Gilmore said. Bless his grumpy, cooking impaired heart.

"I don't know why killing somebody would bother you all of a sudden. We wouldn't even be in this jam if you had kept your cool back in fifty-two."

"That was different. I was only twenty years old, besides Freddy was the one that did the shooting. I didn't even know what was going on until it was over. He did the same thing three years later in Florida, but that time the guard managed to get off a shot and killed

167

him dead."

"Under Texas law you're just as guilty so unless you're interested in visiting our prison facilities down at Huntsville or taking a ride in the electric chair I'd suggest you make sure these boys can't identify you when the time comes."

"I just don't know about this. If you think they need to be killed why don't you do it?"

"I'm a businessman, not a killer. That's what you're being paid to do."

I was suddenly lifted from my place on the porch and slung across someone's shoulder, then carried into the house and back to the same room we'd occupied before. The blindfold was removed after I was put onto the floor and I saw it was Gilmore that'd been carrying me.

He left and returned a moment later with Junebug, who was likewise dumped and then had his blindfold removed.

"Boys, I'm sorry you had to hear all that. But it looks like we haven't got much choice. I can just assure you it'll be as quick and painless as possible."

He looked so pitiful I almost felt sorry for him. Almost.

The voices continued outside for a while, alternating volume as the conversation grew heated then calmed. I kept hoping Gilmore or Freeman would reappear and tell us they'd convinced the third man to let us go, but I knew my only two chances of that were slim and none.

"Joe Ben, we've got to do something."

"No kidding. Any ideas?"

"Yeah, but our timing has got to be just right or we're dead. I think I can get out of these ropes if I can just get my arms slippery enough."

"Are you fixing to hit me in the nose again?"

"No, not this time. Although if all else fails we may have to try that later."

"So what are you gonna do?"

"Nothing much right now. Let's scoot over to where we can push on the boards on the side wall to see if any are loose, but be quiet about it. Once we're sure they're not going to come in and catch us we'll get loose."

I wiggled around until my feet were up against the wall and pushed slowly and firmly against one of the boards. It let out a loud squeak, magnified in the dark and otherwise quiet room as the nail pulled out of the old, dried out wood. I froze in place waiting and expecting to hear the men come running into the room.

I counted to sixty and when there was no response, pushed on the board next to the one I had just tried. It too was loose.

"Junebug, our luck must have changed. The first two I tried were loose."

"Good. That's our way out of here then. Let's scoot back over by the door and wait."

After we'd been laying back in our original positions for a few minutes Junebug whispered to me again.

"Joe Ben?"

"Yeah?"

"You scared?"

"Yeah. Are you?"

"A lot. But if I have to be here with somebody, I'm glad it's you."

"Don't go getting sentimental on me. I wish you were here by yourself."

"I meant if I couldn't have somebody smart here with me, I'm glad it was you."

"Ha ha. Very funny."

We lay there in silence again.

"Joe Ben?"

"Yeah?"

"I know who the third man is."

"How do you know?"

"Did you feel me grab your arm when we were up against the wall?"

"Yeah."

"I was looking out through one of the cracks and I saw him get out of the car."

"Who was it?"

"It was old man Gillespie, from the bank."

# CHAPTER 21

"You're kidding!"

"No I'm not. It was Gillespie all right. As soon as I saw him I knew it was his voice we'd been hearing. I'd have probably caught on sooner or later anyway, he's the only one in town that would say 'a propensity for prevarication', instead of just saying I stretch the truth sometimes."

"I wonder how he got involved in this?"

"Don't you see? These guys were obviously two of the original robbers and the dead one they called Freddy was the third. I figured they knew all about how the bank operated because they were from around here, but I was wrong. It was because they had somebody on the inside, Mr. Gillespie."

"So why would he want to kidnap and kill us?"

"Because of that stupid article in the newspaper. He figured either us or your Uncle Jasper were about to figure things out."

"Why didn't he just run?"

"Too much to lose unless he was sure I guess. By kidnapping us he didn't take as many chances as he would have trying to snatch your uncle and if we really didn't know anything, which we didn't until now, he could just kill us and go on about his business."

"I'll be danged."

We lay there a few minutes contemplating this new turn of events.

"You know what this means though don't you?" Junebug eventually asked, somewhat too cheerfully I thought.

171

"No, what?"

"It means you and me solved a twenty year old mystery that the F.B.I. couldn't even figure out."

"Yeah, this would have sure made us famous. Too bad we'll be dead."

"Just remember what Yogi Bear said, 'It ain't over till it's over'."

"Actually Junebug, it was Yogi Berra, the baseball manager, not Yogi Bear the cartoon."

"Whatever! Here we are in a life threatening situation and you're worrying about who said what. Honestly, Joe Ben I just don't know about you."

\*\*\*\*\*\*\*\*\*\*\*\*\*\*\*\*\*\*\*\*\*\*

We stayed in the room without interruption until the fading light showed it was heading toward evening. Without warning the door suddenly opened and Freeman entered.

"Do you want something to eat?" he asked as he knelt next to us.

We both shook our heads as best we could.

"I just wanted to tell you I'm really sorry. I didn't mean for it to turn out this way. I guess I should have thought it through but then I've never been very good at that. That's why the bank robbery went bad and those people got killed. If I'd have thought to tie them up none of that would have happened. For that mistake I guess I'll end up paying forever."

"It's not too late now. Why make it worse by killing us?" I asked.

"What else can I do? I'm sure y'all are nice kids, but we can't trust you to keep your mouths shut. Matt and I both have wives and families to think about."

"Is that why you killed Ted Duval? Because y'all were afraid he was going to identify you in his book?" Junebug asked.

"What? What are you talking about?" He looked genuinely puzzled.

"Ted Duval. You know the book he was writing was about the robbery, is that why you killed him?"

"I've never seen Ted Duval and hadn't even heard about him until that story in the newspaper."

"Maybe y'all didn't do it, but I bet that other guy had him killed."

"I don't think so. He'd have called us about it rather than bring in somebody else and take the risk of having another person involved. As far as I know, Duval's death didn't have anything to do with us."

He stood up and opened the door again.

"No, I'm sorry boys but there's no other way," he said as much to himself as to us, then shut the door behind him.

"Well, that's that. I guess it's up to us now," Junebug sighed.

"Do you think they'll be coming back in?"

"I doubt it. Both of them will spend the rest of the time convincing each other they don't have any other choice. Then sometime tonight they'll come in here and...you know."

"So what do we do now?"

"We take matters into our own hands. Can you wiggle around and reach into my front pocket?"

"What am I looking for?"

"I've got a leaf in there all wadded up. See if you can pull it out...but be careful."

It took a while but eventually I worked the makeshift package out of his pocket.

"What is this? It feels all squishy."

"It's a wad of grease from the pump on the well. I figured I could use it to work my ropes loose. Try and unwrap the leaf and rub the grease up and down my arms."

We lay there back to back, working blind. A couple of times I had to stop and wait for my hands to uncramp.

"Be careful not to drop it. If you do I'll have to bust you in the nose again."

Eventually I had his arms greased up real good and he commenced to writhing and twisting around. If I hadn't known better I'd have thought he was in the middle of having convulsions or an epileptic fit or something.

After he'd been thrashing back and forth for a while I heard him mutter, "Got it." Within minutes he sat up and I could see his hands were free. In no time at all his feet were also loose.

"Now let's get these ropes off of you and get moving."

He had a little more trouble with my ropes, since the grease was all over his hands and he couldn't get a grip on the knots with his fingers. It seemed like it took forever, but was probably five or ten minutes later when I felt the ropes loosen then drop to the floor.

"That's it. Let's go."

We crawled over to the wall slowly, careful to avoid making any more noise than was absolutely necessary.

"Push the boards out enough to slide through."

I was outside the shack in a mater of seconds, followed closely by Junebug, who meticulously replaced the boards.

"I'd like to see their faces when they try to figure out where we went," he whispered.

"You might have the chance if you don't shut up and hurry. Let's put some distance between us and them."

I started for the woods, careful to keep the cabin between myself and the dog's pen. Luckily, the beast's pen was on the other side so we didn't have to worry about him going crazy as long as we stayed quiet and the wind didn't shift and blow our scent in his direction.

I'd almost reached the tree line when I noticed Junebug wasn't behind me.

My common sense struggled with my loyalty for a moment, but the duty to my buddy eventually won out and I turned back, muttering softly to myself. As I approached the cabin, I saw a shadowy form scoot from under the car.

"What are you waiting on? Let's go," Junebug whispered as he stood and brushed himself off.

It was dark in the trees, but occasionally a ray of moonlight shone through and helped us pick a path through the fallen limbs and trees.

"Which way is it to town?"

"I'm not sure. Which way is the cabin?"

"Back there," I pointed the way we had come.

"Are you sure?"

"Yeah. I've been keeping the moon to my right as we walked."

"Good idea."

"Thanks. Do you know what direction the moon sets in?"

"Do you mean it moves?"

"I'll take that as a no. Let's just find the north star and head that way. That should bring us out to the highway sooner or later."

"Sounds as good as anything else. All I care about is putting as much distance between us and them as possible."

I found the stars that made up the Big Dipper and followed them to find our guiding star. I agreed with Junebug, the direction we went in wasn't as important as the fact that we were going somewhere. I just didn't want to accidentally make a circle and end up back at the cabin.

We'd been walking for two or three hours when I heard what sounded like a gunshot way off behind us.

"Do you think that was them?" I asked as I stopped and bent over trying to get my breath.

"I don't know. I can't think of anybody else who'd be shooting at a time like this."

"What were you doing at their car?"

"I just reached up as far as I could and started yanking stuff loose. I figure even if they get their car started I bought us a little extra time."

I didn't want to waste any more of my precious oxygen by answering so I just reached over and patted him on the shoulder. Even in the dark of the woods I could see the goofy grin I received in response.

We kept walking north, eventually coming to a gravel road just as the sun started lighting up the sky to our right.

"What do you think? Should we stay in the woods or take the road?"

"I feel more comfortable staying in the woods for a while. I think we're better keeping off the roads until we hit one with a lot of traffic."

"Makes sense to me, let's keep going."

We scooted across the gravel and red mud road then into the brush on the other side. After an uncomfortable time pushing our way through the sawbriars bordering the road, we re-entered one of the thick, pine tree forests for which East Texas was famous.

When daylight broke on us, we were following a trail next to a creek. We occasionally stopped and drank, then resumed our pace despite being tired and hungry. I knew when I finally made it home Aunt Sarah would make sure I ate enough to more than make up for the missed meals.

"Let's take a break," Junebug finally said a couple of hours after daylight. We had just came around a bend and saw a big hill sloping upwards in front of us.

I didn't argue, just sat on the trunk of a hickory tree that had fallen across the creek. I wasn't looking forward to that climb any more than he was.

"Do you think we'll be on television?" Junebug asked as he stretched out full length on the tree trunk.

"What?"

176

"When we finally make it back to town. I bet most of the reporters will still be there, do you think they'll put us on the TV news?"

"Junebug, I can honestly say I haven't even considered that. I don't care if I'm ever on television or in the newspaper again. We wouldn't be here now if it wasn't for that last article."

"Yeah, but this is different. We were just spreading a load of bull manure before. This time we've really done something big. We've solved a major crime."

"But we didn't do anything to solve it. All we did was get kidnapped. The criminals did the rest of it."

"Mark my words, that won't matter a bit. All anybody will talk about is that the crooks are finally behind bars. Yup, I believe we'll be mighty famous when this is over. They may even want us to be on one of those television shows about famous people. Shoot, I'll bet.."

"Hush Junebug," I interrupted his musing.

"What?"

"Shhhh. Hush. I heard something."

We waited in silence, straining our ears.

"I don't hear nothing. What do you think you heard?"

I didn't answer, just sat there with my eyes shut focusing on the sounds of the woods.

Suddenly I heard it again and jumped up.

"There it was. Did you hear that?"

"No, what was it? Why've you got that funny look in your eyes?"

"It's a dog barking back the way we came. Sounds like he's pretty close to that road we crossed."

"So? Lots of people have dogs."

"Have you heard one since we left the cabin?"

"No, not that I can remember."

"Neither have I. I don't think we passed any houses all night."

"You don't think it's...," he trailed off as he looked behind us.

"I don't know but I'm not waiting around here to find out."

"Me neither."

We took off at a trot up the hill. If they really were using Hammer the hell hound to trail us I'd be darned if we were going to make it easy on them.

\*\*\*\*\*\*\*\*\*\*\*\*\*\*\*\*\*\*\*\*\*\*\*\*\*

"Faster, Junebug, faster," I hissed as we crawled through a tunnel in a patch of sawbriars. From the looks of the hair caught on the briars to each side and the tracks on the ground it'd been made by wild hogs getting from one side of the creek bottom to the other. I hadn't mentioned what would happen if we met the hogs coming the other way and since Junebug had volunteered to go first I assumed he hadn't thought of it.

We'd crossed the creek at several points, weaving our way back and forth hoping the dog would lose our scent in the water, but apparently to no avail since the occasional bark continued to grow closer.

I knew the briars wouldn't be much of a hindrance to Hammer, but I bet Freeman and Gilmore's skin would have a few reminders of this escapade.

As soon as we came out of the tunnel we stretched our legs and immediately started running again, still following the course of the creek as much as possible.

The dog was close enough behind us to where we could hear him crashing through the underbrush and dry leaves in pursuit of us. I could just imagine the look on his face as he bore down on us, saliva dripping in anticipation of the tender morsels he was tracking. I could only hope that, like a deer, panicked flight would at least make the meat tough and gamy.

"What..do..we..do..now?" Junebug panted as we started up another hill.

"Just keep running and hope he loses the trail or we come to a house or something before he gets to us. Otherwise, we run as long as we can and then climb a tree."

We both looked like we'd been in a war. The dried blood on us from my nosebleeds was now accompanied by fresh from the numerous scrapes and scratches accumulated during our flight through the woods.

As we cleared the next hill I could hear the dog entering the tunnel through the briar patch and knew we only had a few minutes before he would be on us.

Just at that moment we busted through the undergrowth and onto another road, not much different from the first one we'd crossed. We'd nearly made it across when a car suddenly appeared coming around the curve at the end of the road. I just managed to catch a glimpse of the grill before we threw ourselves the last few feet into the underbrush.

"Run Joe Ben, it's them," Junebug screamed. I didn't think we had it in us but we picked up the pace. I heard the car stop and a door slam on the road, then the sound of something else crashing through the bushes and briars. Frenzied barking suddenly erupted behind us as the beast finally caught sight of his prey.

I saw Junebug approaching a brushpile of limbs and branches, then stretching and leaping in an attempt to vault over them without slowing. Unfortunately, his foot caught a limb just at the edge of the pile and he landed on his face, then slid a few feet plowing up pine needles and dirt with his chin before stopping against the trunk of a hickory tree.

I started to slow and help him up but he screamed, "No Joe Ben, keep running. He's right on us."

I took a few more steps and then stopped suddenly and turned to face my attackers, just in time to glimpse the animal launching himself toward me.

# CHAPTER 22

The animal struck me in the chest with his outstretched paws, knocking me backward and causing us both to tumble down the hill end over end. When I stopped rolling I threw up my arms in what I knew would be a futile gesture to ward off the attack.

Before I could shake the dirt out of my eyes I was struck again, but managed to catch the beast's muzzle in both my hands, slowing it slightly as it strove to reach my face, which it did in a split second.

The first lick cleared the dirt out of my eyes but left a trail of slobber from one side of my face to the other. The next twenty or thirty probably cleaned me up as good as I'd been since my last church visit.

"Jake," I yelped and hugged the dog close to my chest, no mean feat considering the contortions he was going through trying to get another lick in.

"Boy, don't you look a sight."

I looked up and saw Uncle Jasper peering over the edge of the drop off, one hand resting on the shoulder of my best friend who was grinning from ear to ear.

"I told you we'd be okay Joe Ben. Just stick with me and I'll keep you out of trouble."

Uncle Jasper laughed as I rolled my eyes.

\*\*\*\*\*\*\*\*\*\*\*\*\*\*\*\*\*\*\*\*\*\*\*\*\*\*

Aunt Sarah and Mrs. Walker spent so much time crying over and kissing on us I thought we'd prune up like you do when you spend too much time in the bathtub.

We ate until we were near to busting, alternating between fried chicken, chicken and dumplings and homemade huckleberry pie. The only bad part of the whole ruckus was when Aunt Sarah insisted on doctoring my cuts and scratches with some kind of red medicine that burned to high heaven.

I was sitting out on the porch with Aunt Sarah still fussing over me when Uncle Jasper meandered up the sidewalk and onto the porch, sitting in his favorite rocker.

"Well, I put out an all points bulletin for those two fellows who kidnapped you. I expect we'll have them before too much longer."

"What about old man Gillespie?" I asked.

"Joe Ben, show some respect. You should call him Mr. Gillespie," Aunt Sarah said out of habit.

"Now Sarah, I'd say that when somebody has you kidnapped and then tries to have you murdered they've given up any claim to your respect. Wouldn't you agree?" Uncle Jasper asked, digging in his pocket for a cigar.

She tried to look stern, then broke into a smile.

"I'd say you're probably right. Old man Gillespie is lucky I don't march up to him and hit him right in the nose." She ran her fingers through my hair as she said this. I had to smile at the thought of Aunt Sarah punching anybody in the nose.

"To answer your question, when I showed up at the bank and put him in the handcuffs, Gillespie broke down and cried like a baby. He confessed to everything. It seems like he'd been embezzling money for years and knew the bank was due for an audit. To hide his theft he hired those three thugs to stage a robbery. What he didn't count on was the bank guard going for his gun and a shootout taking place. He'll be lucky if all he gets is life in prison."

"What'd he say about Ted Duval? Junebug and me kind of figured he had him killed when he found out Duval was writing a book that'd point the finger at him."

181

"That was kind of strange actually. He swears he didn't have anything to do with Duval's death. Said he knew about the book, but thought it was just a general history of the town and the bank robbery was playing a small part in it. He didn't even know Duval was planning on exposing the whole thing until he read it in the newspaper and of course Duval was already dead by then."

"Do you think he was involved?"

"I don't know. He swears he didn't even start trying to contact those South Carolina boys until he read that article about you and Junebug in the paper. The funny thing about the whole deal is that if he hadn't kidnapped y'all then the mystery wouldn't have ever been solved because apparently he destroyed all of the incriminating papers right after the robbery and without an accurate count on the money there was no way to tell he'd been stealing."

"So if he's telling the truth that means whoever killed Duval is still out there."

"That's right. Unless you and Junebug managed to figure that out while you were gone."

"Nope," I heard a familiar voice say from behind me. "But if you'll give us a little bit of time I bet we could. Howdy Joe Ben," Junebug said as he sat on the floor of the porch next to me.

"What've you been doing today?" I asked.

"Oh not much. Just giving interviews about our amazing escape."

"You've been talking to the reporters again? Please tell me you didn't say anything I'll regret later."

"Of course not." He looked at me like I'd said something so ludicrous it really hadn't merited a response at all. "What were y'all talking about?"

We filled him in on the details of the bank president's arrest and collapse.

"I was just asking if old man Gillespie had said anything about killing Mr. Duval. Uncle Jasper said he denied him or those other two having anything to do with it."

"That's what I figured. I don't believe they did."

Uncle Jasper took off his hat and scratched his head, then leaned forward and rested his forearms on his knees twirling his hat around in his hands.

"I know I'm gonna regret this, but on what exactly do you base that astute observation?"

"Do you remember when we were laying on the floorboard in the car and I was flipping stuff out the window?"

"Yeah."

"One of the things I threw out was a paycheck stub with the name Matt Gilmore on it."

"So?"

"I didn't think about it until today, but the paycheck stub covered the last week of May and the first week of June. It showed Gilmore worked a straight fourteen days during the time Duval was killed and dumped in the creek. I don't see how he could have had time to come down here, find Duval, kill him, and then get back to South Carolina in time for work the next day."

"I didn't think I'd ever say this but it appears you thought this thing through Junebug. But tell me, why couldn't it have been the other man?"

"Oh, I guess it could have, but I don't really see why they'd use two people to kidnap two kids and only send one to murder a full grown man."

Uncle Jasper leaned back and rocked for a while.

"I'm curious about how you managed to find us Sheriff. That's not really a place most people would have thought of looking."

"Actually, you can thank your little girlfriend Danielle for a lot of it. She saw you two getting into the car. At first she didn't think much of it, but then she noticed Junebug's hat lying on the ground. She knew he'd never leave it just laying there unless something was wrong so she came and got me."

Junebug looked at me and gloated.

"What'd you do then?"

"I called the state police and had them set cars up on the highways to check for y'all, but when you didn't turn up I knew you were still around here somewhere. So I started driving up and down the roads trying to figure out where you might be."

"Let me guess what happened next. You found the bandana, saw the trail I'd left, followed it to the hide-out then deduced we'd head north and came looking for us." He sat back against the porch post with a smug expression on his face.

"Sorry Junebug, that's not quite what happened. The trail was a good idea but I didn't see any of it." Junebug's expression changed to one of incredulity that his grand scheme hadn't worked as he'd planned.

"Actually I threw Jake into the car and started driving up and down the dirt roads while Cecil stayed here in town going house to house. I took a wrong turn and was driving down this little logging road when Jake went berserk and dove out the window, tearing out through the woods. By the time I stopped the car he was already out of sight."

"I figured he was after a rabbit or a deer, but then I looked down and saw two sets of footprints crossing the muddy road..." His voice trailed off and he stared into space for a moment.

"What's wrong?" I asked.

"Nothing. I almost made a connection right there, but it passed." He shrugged his shoulders. "Oh well, it'll come back to me."

"Like I was saying," he continued. "I knew the tracks were fresh and about the right size for you two so I let Jake run and doubled back so I could drive to the next road over. I figured you'd have left tracks if you crossed that one too. I caught a glimpse of y'all diving

184

into the woods and started to stop just as Jake came tearing past. I followed him and you know the rest."

He stood and put his hat back on and started down the steps. "Well, I guess I'd better move along. Crow doesn't taste any better if you wait."

"What do you mean?" I asked, puzzled.

"I'm going over to the boarding house to apologize to Mrs. Duval. I made a mistake about her and am gonna be a man and 'fess up."

"Can we go with you?" Junebug asked.

"Sure, if you don't mind watching a grown man humble himself."

"It might do them some good Jasper. It would be a good lesson in what happens to somebody who jumps to conclusions."

Uncle Jasper didn't answer, just walked on down the steps and onto the sidewalk, Junebug and I a few paces behind.

\*\*\*\*\*\*\*\*\*\*\*\*\*\*\*\*\*\*\*\*\*\*\*\*

"Well, if it isn't the sheriff and my little friends," Mrs. Duval said when she opened the door. "I'm so glad you two weren't hurt."

She was wearing a white halter top and a red mini-skirt that showed enough of her legs to shame a saloon girl. For a minute I forgot why I was there.

"Mrs. Duval, I'll get right to the point. I'm here to apologize for putting you through the trial and all that..."

"Oh Sheriff," she interrupted him. "You don't have to apologize, you were doing your job. I won't hold a grudge if you won't." She held out her hand.

He clasped and shook it.

"Deal."

As he let go of her hand she looked at me.

"Is something the matter Joe Ben?" she asked.

I realized I'd been standing there staring at her with my mouth hanging open and snapped it shut, biting a good hole in my tongue in the process.

185

"Ouch!" I hollered and started jumping around with my bleeding tongue sticking out.

"Oh my! Let me get some ice for that." She turned and headed for the kitchen, with me tagging behind and trying not to drip on the floor. Between Junebug busting my nose and me nearly biting my tongue plumb in two I'd be lucky if I had enough of my vital fluids left to fill an eyedropper.

Uncle Jasper sat on the sofa in the living room and pulled Junebug down next to him. I failed to see how my pain could provide him with enough amusement to justify the amount of giggling he was doing.

"We'll wait here," Uncle Jasper said.

Mrs. Duval opened the freezer and took out an ice tray, working the lever to break the ice loose. She wrapped a few cubes in a dish towel she got from a drawer and put it against my tongue, taking my hand and putting it against the towel to hold it in place.

"There. That should stop the bleeding in a few minutes."

She held my other hand and led me back into the living room, motioning for me to sit in the chair.

"Just hold that on your tongue for a minute. I was running the water for my bath and I just need to go turn it off."

She smiled at me radiantly and disappeared around the corner. The dull sound of her footsteps on the stairs contrasted with the sharp scent of her perfume that lingered behind.

I heard the water upstairs stop, followed a moment later by the sound of the door closing and her coming back downstairs.

"Now, what brings you here on such a fine day?"

"Mnnph unggl ssedd.." I took the towel away from my mouth.

"Thorry." My tongue felt as swollen as one of those Polish sausages Uncle Jasper liked so much.

"We just wanted to tag along with Uncle Jathper," I lisped out.

"Well, I'm glad you did. I want you to tell me all about your adventure."

Junebug started from when the men had first stopped us with me occasionally throwing in a little morsel of information to fill in the gaps. He'd just gotten to the part where Mr. Gillespie had ordered the two men to kill us when we heard a thump from upstairs, followed immediately by a loud crash from outside.

"What was that?" Uncle Jasper asked as both he and Mrs. Duval jumped up.

"I don't know. Miss Hardeman's at her cafe, we should be the only ones here," she answered as she looked around the corner and up the stairs.

Uncle Jasper grasped her by the arm and stepped around her.

"Let me go first."

He started up the steps, stopping to firmly grab and push Junebug behind him.

He slowly made his way up the stairs and paused at the top, listening. After a moment another muffled 'thump' came from behind the door right next to him. The door that was still marked by a strand of police tape Uncle Jasper had placed over it to keep people out of the last room in which Ted Duval had lived.

He reached down and grabbed the doorknob and twisted.

"It's locked. Do you know where the key is?"

"No. Mrs. Hardeman hid it after she caught one of those reporters trying to open the door with her key ring," she answered.

"Well, I guess the county can afford to pay for a door," he said then kicked the door with his work boot.

The door jumped in the frame and a splintering sound indicated the jamb had cracked. Uncle Jasper put his shoulder against it and pushed, stumbling into the room as the door gave under the force.

Mrs. Duval, Junebug and I crowded through the door to see Uncle Jasper pinning a man to the floor by planting one knee squarely in the middle of his back. As we watched he reached into his rear pocket and produced a set of handcuffs, snapping them around the pinioned fellow's wrists.

"Mr. Lomanto, I presume?"

# CHAPTER 23

"Junebug, run downstairs and call Cecil to bring the squad car over. I think we may finally have who we've been looking for."

Junebug took off like a scalded cat.

"Come on, get up," Uncle Jasper said as he stood, then helped the man get first to his knees, then to his feet.

"Sheriff, I can explain..."

"Son, you keep quiet until the deputy gets here and brings that card so I can read you your rights."

He held the man by the elbow and walked him out of the room past us, careful that he didn't fall when they went down the stairs.

"Now you sit right there until my deputy arrives," Uncle Jasper said as he pushed the man down into one of the overstuffed chairs in the den. "And don't move or you'll force me to forget my manners."

"Yes sir," the man mumbled.

I walked into the other room where Junebug was on the telephone.

"Now why would I do that?" I heard him say into the telephone.

A pause while he listened.

"No, I swear it's the truth."

Another pause.

"Right now, he's got the man in handcuffs."

Pause.

"Of course I'm telling the truth, have I ever lied to you?"

Pause.

"Those times didn't count because I was just kidding."

Short pause.

"Fine, fine, don't believe me, but I'm gonna march right in there and tell him you're not coming because you said you hadn't finished your nap yet."

Shorter pause.

"Good, and I'll expect an apology when you get here."

He hung up the telephone.

"Can you believe he thought I was pulling his leg?" Junebug asked as he turned to me, indignation written all over his face.

"Not you?" I said sarcastically.

He ignored my tone. "Yeah, he said if I made him drive all the way over here for nothing he was gonna paddle my behind. The nerve of some people." He walked into the other room shaking his head. I followed doing the same, although not due to the same person.

Within a few minutes Cecil drove up and we went outside, Uncle Jasper again leading the man by the arm. He placed him into the back of the patrol car and shut the door.

"Now let's go see what that noise was," he said and walked across the yard and around the corner of the house.

"I'll wait here, the yard's so wet from the rain the other night these high heels will sink right in," Mrs. Duval said.

The source of the noise was apparent as soon as we rounded the corner. One of those big aluminum extension ladders was lying on the ground with Uncle Jasper standing next to it staring at the wet turf and the two deep holes that had been gouged in it by the legs of the ladder.

I looked up toward the window of Duval's room and could see two fresh marks where the paint had been knocked off of the window sill by the ladder leaning against it.

190

Junebug began chattering about something, but I was watching my uncle. He had his hat off and was scratching his head again like he did when he was trying to puzzle something out. The cigar he'd thrust into his mouth was working back and forth from one side of his mouth to the other at a feverish pace, getting shorter by the second as he chewed it down. His stare alternated between the ground and the window sill

"Uncle Jasper, what..." I started to ask

"Shhhh," he interrupted.

Junebug had stopped talking and tugged on my shirt sleeve.

"What's he doing?"

"Shhhh," I said. "He's thinking."

Junebug walked over next to my uncle and followed his gaze back and forth between the ground and window. After a few times he changed positions and stood facing my uncle, but on the other side of the marks on the ground. Soon, both of them were moving their heads and eyes back and forth in unison.

Just as I was starting to feel a little hypnotized by the repetitive motions of their heads, Junebug jumped into the air and hollered, "I've got it! I've got it!"

"You've got what?

\*\*\*\*\*\*\*\*\*\*\*\*\*\*\*\*\*\*\*\*\*\*\*\*

"The killer. I know who killed Ted Duval."

Uncle Jasper cocked his head and looked at him.

"Do you still have the pictures you took?"

"Sure do, they're at home."

"Why don't you run get them and bring them here?"

"Right away, Chief." He took off down the sidewalk like a scalded cat.

"What's going on Uncle Jasper?" I was as curious as it's possible for a human to be.

191

"Wait till Junebug gets back. I need to look at the pictures before I'm sure."

He moseyed back to the front of the house, stopping for a moment before he turned the corner to look once more at the ground by the fallen ladder and then again at the window, then continuing on, shaking his head as he went.

"Sheriff, where was Junebug headed in such a hurry?" Mrs. Duval asked as I was walking up.

"Shhhh," Cecil held a finger up to his lips. "You'll jinx it. As long as Junebug Walker is headed away from you it's a good sign." He started chuckling to himself as if he'd said something funny and walked to the car to check on the prisoner again.

"He'll be right back Mrs. Duval. Joe Ben and him took a bunch of pictures the first day we were here and I asked him to go get them."

"Whatever for?"

"Oh, I've got a little brainstorm that might clear up the details on how your husband died."

"Is that right? Can you give me a hint?"

"No ma'am, not just yet." He flopped down onto one of the rocking chairs Mrs. Hardeman had sitting out front. "I would like to know one thing though. How long had you known Mr. Duval had a brain tumor?"

She sat next to him in another chair and looked down at her legs. "I was with him when he found out. He'd been having those blacking out spells and headaches that he swore were going to make his skull split open, so I insisted he see the doctor. They put him in the hospital and ran a bunch of tests, then came in one day with the bad news."

"How'd he take it?"

"How would you react if somebody told you that you were about to die? He got mad at first, then for a little while he wallowed in self pity, not that I could blame him of course. Finally he just squared his shoulders and said he was going to enjoy what time he

192

had left and try to crank out as many books as he could so he'd leave some kind of mark on the world. He was real big on wanting people to remember him. I guess that's because I would have been the only one to really grieve for him when he left. He was disappointed we never had children, but unfortunately I'm not able to. I guess he thought his books would be like his kids would have been, you know, as long as they're around a little part of you is still alive."

I saw a couple of tears roll down her cheeks and drop onto her hands, clasped together in her lap.

"Did he ever discuss what life was going to be like as the tumor grew?"

"One time. He said his greatest fear was that he wouldn't be able to end his days with dignity." She looked up at my uncle. "My husband was a brilliant man, Sheriff. He was always at the top of his class and was well informed on any subject you wished to discuss. I think that's why the tumor was such a blow to him. He was always so proud of his intellect, and then it was as if his brain had betrayed him. The doctors told him his intelligence and perception, or at least his ability to express them, would be kind of like a light bulb with a dimmer switch. Gradually, it would fade until it was no more."

Junebug came running back up just then, carrying a Scooby Doo lunchbox. "My briefcase," he explained, then snapped it open to show a thermos and a stack of photos inside. Uncle Jasper took the box from him and began picking through the pictures, then leaned down and made three rows with several pictures in each.

The first row showed the clearing with the overturned chair and notepad. The next were pictures of the outside of Mrs. Hardeman's house, and the last row contained photographs taken inside Mr. Duval's room before we had touched anything.

He reached into the breast pocket of his coveralls and took out several more pictures, which he added to the rows. From the angle and the fact that each included some portion of Junebug's anatomy I assumed they were from the photos Cecil had taken at the same time Junebug was taking his.

"What do you see here?" Uncle Jasper asked as he looked at me.

"The pictures we took the day after we found the body."

"Look at this one," he pointed to a close up photograph of the writing pad as we'd found it on the ground in the woods.

I stared at it for a minute, then looked up. Junebug was standing next to Uncle Jasper and hopping from one foot to the next like he always did when he was excited. I could tell he knew what my uncle was trying to get at, but I was lost.

"I don't understand what I'm supposed to be looking for."

"Describe the note pad to me."

I shrugged my shoulders. "It's a yellow notepad with a lot of doodles and a few notes made on it. I can't really tell what they say because the ink is smeared so bad."

"Why is the ink smeared?"

"Because it got wet."

He waited a moment, then when it was obvious I still wasn't catching on he asked, "How did it get wet?"

I looked over at Mrs. Duval who had an expression on her face that looked to be a cross between puzzlement and worry.

"I guess it got rained on."

"Exactly."

Junebug couldn't stand being quiet any longer. "Don't you remember Joe Ben? It rained hard the day

194

before we went swimming, that's why the water was so cold."

"So?"

"Please Sheriff, let me explain. Joe Ben isn't ever gonna get it."

Uncle Jasper just nodded his head.

"Don't you see Joe Ben? That rain was the first one we'd gotten in months. So this pad had to have been dropped before or during the rain in order for it to get wet."

"I'm sorry Sheriff, but I must admit I'm as lost as Joe Ben." Mrs. Duval said.

"What Junebug is getting at is what we in law enforcement refer to as a time line. We know that the pad was dropped and got rained on, and since it didn't rain between the time Junebug was talking about and the time we found it we have narrowed the window during which Mr. Duval died and all the events started happening."

"But we already knew that from the coroner's report, and then what Mrs. Duval and Mrs. Hardeman told us about the last time they'd seen Ted Duval," I added.

"That's true, and also if you remember Mrs. Hardeman said he left just as that thunderstorm was about to start because she asked if he needed an umbrella. Doesn't it seem kind of funny to you somebody would get on a bicycle and head off into the woods to write when he knew a storm was brewing?"

Mrs. Duval remained silent, but I said, "I hadn't really thought of it but that is curious."

"Let's look at the rest of these pictures and see what they tell us." He pointed to the bottom row, showing the pictures taken inside the room.

"What do these show?"

I looked closely, trying to figure out the details.

"Well, other than the ones taken by Cecil showing Junebug's big head, they show a room that's been ransacked and piles of wet papers all over the floor next to an open window."

"Exactly, and my head is not big," Junebug said.

"So what does that tell us?"

"That the window was opened either before or during the rainstorm."

"Now look at this picture taken after we'd been in the room for a few minutes."

"There are footprints showing in the wet carpet."

"But there aren't any in the pictures taken before we'd entered. Let's look at this last set of pictures."

I figured that I was looking for something to do with rain and stared at them for several minutes, but nothing clicked. Eventually I looked back up at Uncle Jasper.

"I give up."

"Let me, let me, let me," Junebug burst out.

"Go ahead."

"See this picture here of the outside of the house?"

"Yes."

"That's Mr. Duval's window, right?"

"Yes."

"Now Mr. Duval's door was locked when we got here and Mrs. Hardeman had the only key right?"

"Yes."

"So how would somebody get into the room if they couldn't use the door?"

"Just like that fellow handcuffed in the car, they came in through the window. I bet that's why he came back today, to look around for whatever he couldn't find the first time."

"No, no, no. Look, just follow along for a while. How would he have got to the window to get in?"

I was getting tired of Junebug treating me like I was dim witted. "He flew up there like Dumbo by

196

flapping his ears! You idiot, I just told you he used a ladder just like he did this time."

"Now we're getting somewhere. Take this picture of the window and go and compare it to the window today and tell me what's different."

I did and returned a few seconds later.

"The ladder left marks on the painted window sill."

"So what does that tell you?"

"That it didn't before."

"Now take this picture," he handed me one of the pictures Cecil had taken, "and go look and compare this right here," he pointed at a spot."

"Why should I compare your ear?"

"No, not my ear. Cecil is about as much a photographer as my granny is, anybody could have taken pictures without always putting me in them. Look here just to the left of my ear, now go compare that."

He wanted me to look at a place on the lawn.

I returned slower this time, mentally reviewing what I'd seen.

"Do you get it now?" he asked.

"Yeah, I think so."

"Would you mind explaining it to me then?" Mrs. Duval asked as she put her hand on my shoulder.

"When that fellow crawled up there today he used a ladder and left gouge marks and footprints all over the yard because it's so wet and muddy. But look at that picture," I handed it to her. "There aren't any marks or footprints visible, so that means there wasn't a ladder used and nobody was walking on the yard after it got wet. Since we've already determined your husband left right as it started raining that means the window had to have been opened and the room ransacked while he was here."

"I don't understand."

Uncle Jasper spoke up. "Mrs. Duval, it seems that your husband was the one that opened his window and tore up the room."

# CHAPTER 24

"Why would he do that?" She stammered out.

Junebug was looking at her curiously, with the eyebrow over his gotch-eye cocked.

"I was hoping maybe you could explain that for me," Uncle Jasper said.

"What do you mean?"

"Well Mrs. Duval, I've got a feeling you know more than you're letting on.

"Sheriff, I don't know what you're talking about."

"There are a lot of things about this case that just don't add up..."

He was interrupted by Cecil running up, or at least doing what he called a run.

"Sheriff, that man out there in the car..." he stopped speaking and leaned over to catch his breath.

"Cecil, you're going to have to lay off the fried chicken and mashed potatoes every day for lunch. It's embarrassing to have a deputy who can't run more than four steps without having to stop and catch his breath."

"All..right..Sheriff." He gulped in air for a moment and then stood up. "That man in the car, he claims his name is Larry Hobson and he's a reporter. I checked his wallet and he's got an I.D. card from a Dallas paper. He even had a clipping of one of the articles he'd written with his picture next to it."

"Come with me," Uncle Jasper held his arm out for Mrs. Duval, who took it in her hand and then tagged along as he walked to the patrol car and opened the back door.

"All right, what's going on?" he asked the man in the back.

"I was snooping around trying to find a new lead on the story. The lady that owns the boarding house wouldn't let me look through Duval's room so I decided to sneak in and take some pictures, maybe turn up something y'all missed. Unfortunately, I tripped over a pile of papers when I climbed into the room."

"Are you sure that's the truth?"

"Of course. Look Sheriff, I know it was wrong, but I was just looking for a new angle on a story. You can call my editor at the paper and he'll verify my assignment."

"Where were you when Duval died?"

"I was on assignment in Los Angeles from the first part of May until late June. I can prove that too."

Uncle Jasper scratched his head.

"All right Cecil, take Mr. Hobson down to the jail and lock him up while you check out his story. If everything is as he says it is, write him a ticket for trespassing and let him go."

He slammed the door, then watched as Cecil drove away with the prisoner in the back.

"How do you know you didn't just release my husband's murderer?" Julia Duval asked.

"Mrs. Duval, I guarantee you that man didn't have anything to do with your husband's death," Junebug piped up. "The man that killed your husband is dead....but, then you already knew that didn't you?"

I stared at my friend in amazement.

"Junebug, what are you saying?"

"Young man, it sounds like you still think I murdered my husband."

"No ma'am, I don't. What I do believe is that you know who actually is responsible."

"Why do you say that?"

"There are too many things in this case that don't match up, things that indicate Ted Duval wasn't doing what everybody thinks he was."

"For instance?"

"Well, to start off, everybody says he needed to wear his glasses when he was doing his writing, and yet the glasses were buttoned in his shirt pocket."

"What does that prove?"

"Nothing by itself, but there was also all of those superstitions he had. You and his agent told us he never typed up his work until he was completely finished, yet we found a typed first page of his book even though he'd told Mr. Goldman he was still a week away from being through. The lucky pen he insisted on using was buttoned in his shirt pocket as well, even though the notepad was lying on the ground as if it had fallen there when the drug took effect and the chair overturned."

"There's also the matter of the trail leading to the creek," Uncle Jasper interjected. "I found the limb that was used to brush the footprints from the trail, but it was in the creek. Obviously whoever used it worked their way from the woods to the water, not vice versa, yet no footprints led away from the edge. Interestingly, the pocketknife in your husband's pocket had pieces of wood around the blade."

"I don't see what you're getting at Sheriff."

"One more thing Mrs. Duval, the handprint we found in the dirt at the end of the trail. It was like somebody in the water had been in the creek and had held onto the bank."

"What is your point?"

"My point is the person who killed your husband died at the same time he did."

"But you only found one body."

"Exactly. Because your husband and the killer were one and the same. He committed suicide."

\*\*\*\*\*\*\*\*\*\*\*\*\*\*\*\*\*\*\*\*\*\*\*\*\*\*\*\*\*

"Why would he do that?"

"That's what I hope you can tell us. I can understand and explain the suicide, after all he knew he

201

was going to die a slow and painful death from the tumor. What I can't understand is why he went to these lengths to disguise it. Plus, he had to know that everybody would be suspicious of your involvement. If he truly loved you why would he put you in that kind of jeopardy?"

I was still staring with my mouth open as Mrs. Duval looked at the ground. Her shoulders started shaking and soon sobs escaped her. I didn't know what else to do so I walked over and hugged her around the waist.

Eventually she quit crying and looked back up at my uncle.

"He did love me very much, I know that for sure. From the way he'd been talking, when I left that day I suspected I was seeing him for the last time. He said that if anything ever happened to him, he had something he wanted me to give to somebody when the time was right. He also said I'd know when and who. I'll be right back."

She turned and walked up the sidewalk and entered the house.

"When did you figure all of this out?" I asked Junebug.

"Today, while we were standing out here looking around. I was looking at the ladder marks and all of a sudden everything meshed, and I realized Duval had to be the one that messed up his room. It was just a short leap from there to the suicide."

Uncle Jasper grinned at Junebug and said, "I should have seen it sooner, but I was proceeding on the assumption it was a murder. That's what happens when you don't keep an open mind."

The front door slammed and Julia Duval walked back to us carrying an envelope in one hand and a handkerchief in the other. She handed the envelope to Uncle Jasper.

"I had it hidden in the binding of one of my books of poetry. I've been tempted to open it many times, but Ted was so emphatic that it was only to be opened in a very specific circumstance that I didn't."

Uncle Jasper used his pocketknife to cut the top of the envelope open, then withdrew several folded sheets of paper, covered with words which I suspected had been written by Mr. Duval using his lucky pen.

My uncle stared at the paper for a moment, then began reading:

To Whom It May Concern:

Congratulations and curses upon you.

As you probably know by now, I am dead as a result of overdosing on Dalmane and then placing myself in Sandy Creek, where I drowned.

If you are reading this letter it means either you've solved the mystery or my wife is about to be found guilty of my murder.

I think she suspected what I was going to do, but I never told her. The pills I took were my own prescription, given to me by Dr. Weinberg in Oklahoma City. I want to make it clear that Julia did not aid or abet in any way in what I am doing.

You may wonder why I went to all this trouble rather than just shooting myself or even just swallowing a bottle of the pills and lying down to go to sleep.

It's actually very simple and very vain. I want to be remembered. What better way for a mystery writer to die than being murdered in an unsolved crime? This would have assured me a place in literary history.

Unfortunately, it appears I am even less of a real mystery creator than I am a real mystery solver. I intended for my final book to be the solution to the St. John bank robbery, but must admit I am no closer to solving it than when I started. I originally suspected it was an inside job, and was even suspicious of a loan officer named Hiram Gillespie, but have been unable to find anything to support my theory. I guess Julia will have to return the publisher's advance money.

If you've gotten to this point you either know already or will know shortly there is no such person as Joshua Lomato. I made him up just so we'd have another suspect. So that there will be no doubt I was the one that actually wrote this letter I have placed a duplicate with my attorney, Andrew Valone, in New York City.

I wanted this mystery to be my legacy for the future. I suspect that it will be solved one day, but hopefully not until a chance for the mystique to be built up around my death.

Now why suicide in the first place? That is an even easier question. I couldn't bear the thought of what was to come. I didn't fear death or the impending discomfort so much as I dreaded the thought of losing my ability to think and express myself. That was my greatest terror.

Tell Julia I love her very much and was sorry I couldn't be a better husband, but it just wasn't in me. She is my first and only true love and I'm sorry everything had to end this way.

I hope that whoever is reading this letter will consider a request that this mystery remain a mystery is really a dying man's last wish. But I understand you have to do what is necessary.
Always,
Duval

We all stood in silence for a while, thinking about the events of the last few months.

"You know, of course, it wouldn't be right for you to keep the insurance money?"

"I don't care about the money, I've got more of it than I'll ever be able to use."

"I'm sure there are some wonderful charities out there that could use the money," I added.

"I was just thinking, everything we've talked about today is just a theory isn't it? I mean there is no real proof there was a suicide."

"Other than that letter," Junebug reminded him. He handed the envelope and pages back to her.

"What are you going to do now?" she asked.

"Oh, I'll keep investigating but I imagine this will go on the books as an unsolved crime. It's kind of funny though..."

"What is?"

"Before this started I only had one unsolved crime in the entire time I've been sheriffing, the bank robbery. Now that one is solved, you could say because of your husband's death, and we have another one on the books to take its place. It's a fair trade I guess."

"Do you mean...?"

"Yes ma'am. As far as I'm concerned Ted Duval was murdered by a person or persons unknown and apparently undiscoverable. That'll be the official position on the file. When you add that to the fact these two young 'uns solved the bank robbery due to being involved in Ted Duval's investigation I can almost assure you his place in history is established."

She sniffed and looked at Uncle Jasper with those beautiful blue eyes.

"Thank you Sheriff, for me and for Ted. A person should leave something behind for others when they die. This and his books are Ted's legacy."

"I know how you feel," he rubbed my head and squeezed my shoulder. "I just hope I'm remembered after I go."

"You will be Uncle Jasper, I promise."

"Me too. I hope everybody remembers me," Junebug chimed in.

"Junebug, I can assure you that for one reason or another you will certainly make your mark on this world. I only hope the world survives it."

\*\*\*\*\*\*\*\*\*\*\*\*\*\*\*\*\*\*\*\*\*\*

"Not a bad summer, all in all was it Joe Ben?" Junebug asked as we sat on the porch the afternoon before the first day of school.

"Nope, it was definitely exciting."

"You know. I bet there aren't a lot of kids that had a summer anywhere near as cool as ours."

"That's for sure."

We didn't talk for a while as I sat there reflecting on the events of our vacation.

"Junebug?"

"Yeah?"

"How are you and Danielle doing?"

"Not so good actually."

I looked over at him digging at the bottom of his shoe with his pocketknife.

"What happened?"

"The newspapers got all excited about her being the one who found my hat and set your uncle to looking for us. After the third or fourth story she got the big head, and I just couldn't live with it."

"Oh." I suspected that what that translated to was Junebug was jealous of the attention Danielle was getting.

"You know what else?"

"What?

"I never did get my fried catfish."

"So?"

"I was thinking, we could run out to the creek today and try to grab some fish like I was telling you about."

"Nope, you just keep thinking. I don't know if I could stand another episode like we've been through."

"Yeah, maybe you're right. We'll just get the poles and see what we can catch next weekend."

"Okay."

The screen door slammed just then and Uncle Jasper walked out on the porch.

"You boys look like you're in deep thought."

"Just thinking about this summer and how much fun it was," I said.

"I'm afraid this school year is going to have a hard time keeping up with our summer, don't you think so?" Junebug asked.

"I'd have to agree."

"I'm afraid you and Cecil will be bored to tears without any excitement or mystery to keep you busy."

Uncle Jasper looked amused for a moment.

"Junebug, there is one thing in this world I'm sure of. There will never be a lack of excitement in my life as long as you two are around."


THE END

## About the Author

Robert D. Bennett was born in Louisiana and spent his childhood there and in Texas.

His diverse work history has taken him across the United States, Mexico and the Caribbean as well as England, and his books are shaped by the people he has known and the places he has visited.

"If I write about a place, it's because I've visited there and either the place or the people left an impression", Bennett said when asked about the inspirations for his books.

He currently resides in Texas with his wife Karren and his Jack Russell Terrier "Sup" and occasionally his twin sons as they return from college on breaks and his daughter and son in law when they visit.

Coming Soon

Look for more titles in the Junebug series by this author at www.RobertDBennett.com or follow him on
Twitter at RoberttheWriter